P9-DNM-865

THE
GHOST
OF
RAMSHAW
CASTLE

By Robert Sutherland

Cover by Laura Fernandez

Scholastic Canada Ltd.

Scholastic Canada Ltd.
123 Newkirk Road, Richmond Hill, Ontario, Canada L4C 3G5

Scholastic Inc.
730 Broadway, New York, NY 10003, USA

Ashton Scholastic Pty Limited
PO Box 579, Gosford, NSW 2250, Australia

Ashton Scholastic Limited
Private Bag 1, Penrose, Auckland, New Zealand

Scholastic Publications Ltd.
Villiers House, Clarendon Avenue,
Leamington Spa, Warwickshire CV32 5PR, UK

Canadian Cataloguing in Publication Data

Sutherland, Robert, 1925-
    The ghost of Ramshaw Castle

ISBN 0-590-73286-2

I. Title.

PS8587.U798G48   1989   jC813'.54   C88-095301-2
PZ7.S87Gh 1989

7 6 5 4 3   Printed in Canada   2 3 4 5/9
Manufactured by Webcom Limited

For Shona, Bonnie, Struan and Grace
who love books

1

"I don't remember ever hearing that Ramshaw Castle was haunted."

"I'm not saying it is, David." Sandy's voice sounded as clear as if she were speaking to him from across the room instead of across the ocean. "I'm just saying strange things have been happening."

"Oh? What sort of things?"

"Lights where there shouldn't be any lights. Smoke from the chimney of an empty building. Noises in the night. That sort of thing."

"Well," said David, "when you're talking about a building that's — what? seven, eight hundred years old? — it seems reasonable to assume it might be haunted."

"There was said to be a ghost at one time," Sandy admitted. "But she hasn't been seen for more than a hundred years."

"Tell me about her."

1

"On a long distance call? No way. I'd better get to the reason I called."

"You don't have to have a reason," David assured her. "Call anytime. For instance, if you should actually have two consecutive days without rain . . . "

"Don't joke about our weather," she chuckled. "If we didn't have plenty of rain I probably *wouldn't* be talking to you. I'm calling to offer you a job for the summer."

"A job!" David was both intrigued and mystified. "Let me guess. You want me to solve the mystery of the ghost of Ramshaw Castle before the rain washes away all the evidence."

"No, no." Sandy was laughing out loud now. "All that talk about strange happenings was just to whet your appetite. Do you know anything about gardening?"

David shook his head in bewilderment. "Not a thing. What —"

"Good. Then you can start from scratch when you get here," she told him.

"Anytime you'd care to explain what you're talking about would be fine with me," David said with feeling.

Sandy chuckled, then took pity on him.

"You know that Ramshaw Castle has been empty for the last couple of years, ever since we managed to get the Laird shipped off to prison."

David's mind flew back to that summer when he had met Sandy. Together they had thwarted the Laird of Ramshaw's plans to sell a deadly bacillus to terrorists who could have held the world for ransom.

"Well, the National Trust has now taken the castle over," Sandy continued. "It's going to be open to the public, with several rooms to be used as bed-and-breakfast units. I've been hired as one of the guides to take tourists around the castle and grounds and tell its story. And the head gardener tells me he's going to need some help because of the luxuriant growth brought on by that abundance of rain you were joking about. I told him I knew someone who would be perfect for the job. What do you think?"

"I'm already packing." David's answer was out almost before Sandy finished speaking. "When do I start?"

"The first of June." The delight in her voice matched the excitement in his.

§ § §

It happened with such suddenness that the startled guards had little time to react. The helicopter shot up from the shelter of the nearby trees and swept in over the prison wall, rotors clattering.

The men in the exercise compound looked up in surprise. But one of them was ready and waiting. At the first sound he darted from the column that had been marching to the drill-like commands of a guard, and ran to the centre of the yard. A rope fell from the open door of the helicopter. He grabbed it, scrambling feet searching for and finding stirrups. Then he was winched up, even as the aircraft moved off. For a moment it seemed that there had been a miscalculation, that his body, swinging like a pendulum, would smash against the prison wall. But he cleared it by a few centimetres.

Only then did the gunfire begin, from a guard on the ground, and a sentry in the tower, but it was too late, too erratic. With the man still swinging from the rope and nearing the body of the aircraft, the helicopter ducked down behind the trees once more.

As the man climbed in, they flew low along a valley, treed hills sweeping away on either side, patchwork fields below. Dusk was gathering down there.

The pilot merely glanced at the newcomer. "Welcome aboard," he said.

"Thanks. Beautiful flying."

The pilot grunted an acceptance of the compliment. As he pulled the aircraft up over a hill, headlights blinked twice down below. The helicopter settled gently in a field near the road.

The escaped convict opened the door, slapped the pilot lightly on the shoulder, and moved away into the gloom. He climbed a stone dike to reach the car where it waited, door open. A moment later the car was moving fast, the helicopter forgotten.

Twice more he changed vehicles. The third

car finally pulled off a busy motorway into a treed lane, and eventually stopped at a farmhouse. The man got out, spoke a word of thanks to the driver, then turned to go in.

Another man was coming out of the house to grip the newcomer's hand. "Welcome back, Ramshaw."

The man thus addressed grinned and shook his head. "Forget that name. As owner of the castle I was once called the Laird of Ramshaw, but that's all over now. I'm just plain William Fletcher. And if you've arranged things as we planned, *that's* over too."

"Right you are." The other man led the newcomer into the house. "You'll go out of here a completely different man. But for now, how about a drink?"

"Sounds good, Jake. Whiskey and soda if you have it, please."

Moments later the two men were relaxing in easy chairs. Jake looked across at the escaped prisoner. He was a well-built man of medium height who had obviously maintained top physical condition in prison. The grey was perhaps a little more prevalent in his hair and in his clipped, military mustache, but it detracted nothing from his vigorous appearance. He took a pipe from his pocket and began to fill it, pressing the tobacco down into the bowl with a blunt thumb.

"Yes," Jake spoke with satisfaction, "everything is planned. Your forged papers are already prepared except for a passport photograph. Once Henri is done with you, we'll add that and you'll be a totally new man."

"Henri?"

"Our make-up artist. He's good. With a few touches here and there he'll change your appearance so even I won't know you."

"When will he begin?"

"Right now, if you like. He's anxious to get a look at you."

A few moments later Henri stood before the escaped prisoner, studying the former Laird of Ramshaw with critical enthusiasm.

"Well," said the latter lightly after a long moment, "what do you think? Would a fake beard and wig not be sufficient?"

Henri remained serious. It was another long moment before he shook his head. "We are not amateurs," he replied slowly. "We do not use fakery, though in some cases real beards are a good disguise. When did you grow your moustache?"

The other was taken by surprise. "When? I don't remember."

"No, of course not. You cannot remember when you did not have one, *n'est-ce pas*? Faces like yours demand moustaches. You will feel naked without one. Nevertheless it must go. That alone will be make a big difference.

"A short beard then? Maybe, we shall see. Certainly a new jaw line, a reshaped nose. Don't be alarmed, it's quickly and easily done. And, of course, contact lenses to change the colour of your eyes. Built-up shoes to alter your height, perhaps. Oh, yes, you are a fine subject.

"Tell me, are you likely to be spending much time with people who knew you before? Besides Jake, of course."

"No, he won't." It was Jake who spoke, firmly, as if expecting an argument. "It's all arranged. He's going to Canada to head up a new operation there. We've already picked out the place in Ontario."

But the former Laird waved him to silence. He turned to Henri. "Why do you ask?"

"Because if so, you must change any habits or mannerisms you might have. We cannot work miracles in so short a time. A casual glance will fool anyone, but if for some reason someone who knew you before begins to suspect, then a familiar habit might be all it takes to give you away."

The other thought for a moment, then shook his head. "I don't think I have any habits like that. What do you think, Jake?"

"It doesn't matter," Jake answered irritably. "You won't be meeting anyone in Canada who knew you before."

"Maybe not," agreed Ramshaw, "but I'm not going to Canada just yet. First" — he spoke firmly, looking at Jake — "I have some unfinished business to attend to in Lewis. At Ramshaw Castle."

2

It was a rare day, sunny and warm, when David saw Ramshaw Castle again. Beyond a low hill, the castellated tower was outlined against the sky as the taxi came round a bend in the road. David leaned forward to touch the driver on the shoulder.

"Stop here, please. I'll walk the rest of the way."

Standing on the edge of the road, he considered his plan of approach. The summer before, Sandy had surprised him by arriving in Canada ahead of schedule and catching him off guard. Now he was about to return the compliment. She wasn't expecting him for two days yet.

He left the road and walked over open moorland. At the crest of the hill he paused. Before him stood the castle. The rear part, dominated by an ancient stair tower, was in picturesque ruin, but the forepart of the original structure was still in good repair. A new wing had been added in the last century, including, as David was well aware, a library, drawing rooms and a modern kitchen on the main floor, and a number of bedrooms and servants' quarters on the floors above.

A well-kept lawn bordered by flower beds and a car park lay between the castle and the road. Beyond the building, heath sloped away on all sides, except to the rear where a headland loomed. Far to the south blue water gleamed in the sunlight, and beyond it the purple hills of Harris shouldered into the sky.

Here and there over the expanse of moorland white sheep grazed. Unsightly huts offered temporary shelter to shepherds and peat cutters. A plume of smoke ascended from a lonely croft, the only sign of habitation in a desolate land.

A movement from across the vista caught David's eye. A bus appeared, approaching on the winding road. A tour bus, he guessed, for this road was not on any regular bus line. Headed for the castle? Three cars already stood in the parking lot, and several people were gathered nearby as if waiting for something. David glanced at his watch. Perhaps there was to be a conducted tour on the hour, in twenty minutes. If so, he could merge with the tourists and watch for an opportunity to surprise Sandy.

The bus and David arrived at the parking lot almost together, and he merged easily with the twenty or so people who climbed out. Chattering voices in a number of different languages surrounded him, but all became silent as the door of the castle opened and a kilted piper appeared.

He was an old man, erect and proud in his highland garb. The sunlight sparkled from the jewelled clasp on his shoulder, the ornaments on his sporran and *sgian dhu*. He stood gazing at the distant hills for a moment, then struck up a lively tune and began to march across the pavement in front of the door.

Aulay MacLure. David remembered him well from his previous visit to Ramshaw Castle. He worked his way forward through the throng, wondering if MacLure would recognize him. But the piper was lost in his music and payed little attention to his audience. Even their enthusiastic applause went unrecognized.

The performance lasted for several minutes, ending with "Scotland the Brave." The last notes were still lingering when the castle door opened again and Sandy appeared.

David watched her for a moment with a warm glow in the region of his heart. He remembered her in many roles and many costumes: a barefoot deckhand on her uncle's trawler; a lady of honour in a gown of French silk gracing the great hall of Ramshaw Castle; in a sweater and jeans, paddling a canoe in the wilds of Algonquin Park. And now here she was in something different — a simple white blouse and kilted tartan skirt.

But the reddish brown curls that caught the

sunlight and her sparkling blue eyes were the same as ever. David looked at her for only a moment, then turned away and edged back into the throng before she could see him. He pulled the front of his baseball cap down over his eyes and stood close to the shelter of a wide-brimmed hat worn by an American lady.

"Good morning, ladies and gentlemen. Welcome to Ramshaw Castle." Her clear voice carried to the far edge of the crowd, its highland lilt warm and welcoming. "We are about to start on a tour of the castle. Please stay as close to me as possible so you will be able to hear. At the end of the tour you will be welcome to roam the castle or grounds on your own if you wish. We ask only that you do not open any closed doors or pass any danger signs. Parts of the castle have not been looked after for hundreds of years and are not safe."

"Hundreds of years!" murmured David's American neighbour in awe. "Did you hear that, Wally?"

"We also have a guest book here and would appreciate it if each of you would sign it before you leave. Ah, I see some of you have already done so. Good." Sandy glanced down at the open page. "We have three people from Oldenburg, Germany. Where are you, please?"

Three young people, two boys and a girl in hiking gear, held up their hands.

"*Ceud mile failte.* Welcome to the Hebrides.

11

We hope you enjoy your stay in Scotland." Sandy turned to the book again.

"Captain Reginald Moss, Royal Navy, retired."

David saw an erect man with a military bearing and a short black beard wave one hand. Sandy smiled and nodded at him.

"Timothy Stevens, of London." Mr. Stevens stood slightly above-average in height in spite of an abundance of camera gear hung about his person.

"Ah, this is interesting," Sandy continued. "We have a Mr. and Mrs. Wallace Morrison of Toledo, Ohio."

"That's us, Wally!" the American lady squealed in delight. "Wave, Wally." David turned his face away quickly lest Sandy should spot him. He edged carefully to one side.

"Were you aware," Sandy was saying to the Americans, "that this was Morrison country for hundreds of years, and that this castle was built by the Morrisons of Ramshaw? Were your ancestors Scottish, Mr. Morrison?"

"Yes." Wally's face was almost as red as the colourful shirt he wore. "My great-grandfather came from the mainland. From the west coast, I believe."

"But *his* ancestors probably came from Lewis. Many of the Morrisons were driven off the islands to the mainland in the seventeenth century. We're glad you're here, Mr. Morrison.

"I should mention before we begin the tour," Sandy continued, turning slightly to address the entire company again, "that we have a bed-and-breakfast operation here now. If any of you wish to stay in the area, you can book one of the bedrooms on the second floor. Your fee will include a hearty highland breakfast in the great hall."

"Oh, Wally, let's stay one night at least. After all, we're Morrisons and this is a Morrison castle." The American lady barely waited for her husband's assent. "Miss. Oh, Miss . . . "

"My name is Sandy MacLeod. Please just call me Sandy. What is it, Mrs. Morrison?"

"Can you put us down for a night or two? We'd love to stay."

Sandy smiled an acknowledgement. "We'll take care of the bookings at the end of the tour," she said. "But don't worry, Mrs. Morrison, I'll make sure there's a room for you. Now if you'll follow mo . . . "

David moved with the group in Sandy's wake, dodging behind the others to avoid her eye, yet staying close enough to hear the anecdotes she told about the castle's past.

The original castle was built in the fourteenth century, she explained, and was involved for many years in clan battles with the neighbouring MacLeods and MacKenzies. Yet its one ghost had nothing to do with those battles.

"It happened over there." Sandy pointed to

13

the old stair tower that rose twenty metres above the crumbling wall of the original wing. "The lady of the house fell from the top of the tower to her death. Her husband, the Laird, was devastated by the accident and vowed that such a thing would never happen again. In his grief he had the tower sealed off forever, with an iron-barred yett, or gate, embedded in the walls to bar any entrance to the tower. As you can see beyond that wall, it's still there today, and no one has entered the tower since that day. No one, that is, except the spectre of the lady herself."

Those words brought forth a storm of excited queries. "Is she the ghost? What does the ghost look like? Does it appear often?"

Sandy was well prepared to answer the questions. "Apparently the ghost looked enough like the lady who fell to leave no doubt as to its identity. But I'm afraid it hasn't been seen — officially, anyway — since the Morrisons sold the castle."

Not officially, thought David, but *something* has been seen since. What had Sandy said? "Lights where there shouldn't be any lights." What could have caused them?

But apparently Sandy wasn't going to mention the mysterious lights to these tourists. She continued to move on, and soon began another tale that caught everyone's imagination. In spite of being surrounded by more powerful enemies, the Morrisons had clung tenaciously to their castle until the early nineteenth century, when harsh economical conditions finally forced them to sell out.

"The tragedy was," explained Sandy, "that they shouldn't have had to sell out at all. Two hundred years previously, the MacKenzies had paid the Laird a fortune in diamonds as ransom for their heir who had been taken captive. Sale of the diamonds would have made the Morrisons wealthy indeed, but before they could be sold, the diamonds disappeared."

"Disappeared!" echoed Timothy Stevens, the man with the cameras. "How can a fortune in diamonds disappear?"

"No one knows," admitted Sandy. "There are theories, of course. The generally accepted explanation is that one of the sons of the Laird stole them and hid them somewhere. But he was killed in battle a few days later, and to this day they have never been found. Or if they have been, the finder never admitted it."

"Do you mean to say," exclaimed the American woman, all excited, "that the diamonds might still be here somewhere? If they are, they would be Morrison property, wouldn't they? Do you hear that, Wally? You're a Morrison."

But her husband shook his head. "Hush, Irene. They've nothing to do with us. We're not of this branch. And besides, I expect they would belong to whoever bought the castle from the Morrisons."

"Oh, no! Is that true, Miss — Sandy?"

Sandy laughed. "The question is academic," she said. "I suppose the courts would have to decide what to do with them, but I'm sure they were found long ago by someone who kept them for himself without bothering to tell anyone. Perhaps the people who owned the castle before the National Trust took over found them."

"Who were they?"

"People by the name of Fletcher. The castle was bought from the Morrisons by William Fletcher, an industrial tycoon. He restored the great hall and one tower of the original castle, and added a new wing tastefully designed to blend in with the old. His grandson, another William, was the last Fletcher to own the castle. He brought dishonour to the family — and on the old building — by leading a vast network of smugglers and terrorists. He was caught only two years ago, and is currently living out a long sentence in prison."

By this time the group had followed Sandy through the entrance and into the great hall. Here the morning light filtered through high, narrow slits, turning the eyes of a mounted stag's head into pools of fire and winking off the blades of a pair of claymores over the huge fireplace. The hall was dominated by a massive table covered with a snow-white cloth and bearing silver candlesticks at intervals.

"It would add romance to the castle," said

Sandy, "if I could say that Bonnie Prince Charlie slept here, but he never did. He did, however, dine here in this room at this very table." A chorus of "oohs" and "ahs" greeted her revelation.

"Actually," she added, "he was not welcome at all. He was in flight from his enemies, and the Laird of Ramshaw at the time was not one of his supporters. He gave him food because highland hospitality demanded it, but he bustled him out the door as soon as he had eaten, and was relieved to see the back of him."

The majority of the crowd obviously disapproved of this callous act, and the American woman was heard to remind those nearby that she was only a Morrison by marriage, and besides, by that time Wally's people had moved to the mainland. But by now the thought uppermost in the minds of the tourists was anticipation of a chance to explore the castle.

"This is the end of our guided tour," Sandy announced, "but please feel free to enjoy the castle and grounds on your own now. I'm sorry that as yet we do not have a tea room or gift shop, but don't forget our bed-and-breakfast option. Thank you all for your interest and patience. I will be available for a while to answer any questions you may have. Please don't forget to sign our visitors' book before you leave."

As the crowd began to split up, David edged behind Sandy. Removing his cap, he touched her on the shoulder and spoke softly.

"One question, Miss MacLeod. What are your plans for lunch?"

She turned, and for a moment it was there — a flash of surprised and delighted recognition. Then it was gone, but he had seen it and was satisfied.

"I don't know, really," she said after a pause, speaking for the benefit of those lingering nearby. "Perhaps I could find the answer to your question in the library, if you are interested. If we don't know an answer, we always do our best to find it."

"What was the question?" demanded a fussy Englishwoman. "I couldn't hear what he said."

"Oh, he — well, he wanted to know — ah — where Bonnie Prince Charlie went when he left here. And I'm sure the answer lies in one of the books in the library." She turned to David. "If you're in no hurry, Mr. — What's your name?"

"David McCrimmon," he answered gravely, "from Woodstock, Ontario, Canada."

"Oh, yes," she said, equally solemnly, "the town with the cow. The library is the first door on your right, Mr. McCrimmon. Why don't you go ahead, and I'll join you there in a moment."

"If you're sure it's no bother," David's eyes twinkled. "Thank you very much."

§   §   §

It wasn't long before Sandy joined him in the library, pulling the door behind her.

18

"Were you there in the crowd all that time?" she demanded.

He nodded, grinning. "I kept my hat pulled down and made sure you didn't see me. You're a very good guide."

"Thank you." For a moment they stood looking at each other. Then she ran and was caught up in his arms.

"Gee, Sandy," he said, breathlessly, "it's good to see you again."

"You too." She kissed him lightly, and he let her go reluctantly. "I suppose now you've paid me back for surprising you in your store at Little Bear Lodge."

"That's right, we're even now. And I still want to know the answer to my question."

"Well," she said gravely, "I plan to have lunch in the kitchen with the staff. You're not expected until Saturday, but I'm sure we can scrape up enough haggis and neeps for you too."

"Thanks a lot! If it's really haggis you're having, I'll pass."

"No, no, I was just kidding. I expect it will be meat pies and chips. Anyway — " She paused as a knock sounded at the door. It was the English tourist.

"Did you find the answer to the young man's question?"

"Oh, yes." Sandy waved her hand to encompass the books that seemed to be everywhere. "We can find the answer to almost any question thrown at us if we have time."

"So, what is it? The rest of us would like to know too."

For a moment Sandy couldn't remember what question she had invented. Then she brightened.

"Where did the Prince go? He went on from here to Stornoway and spent the night there with loyal followers. That was just before he escaped to France."

"Really? Oh, well, thank you." The woman spoke begrudgingly and looked at the two of them suspiciously before she left.

David grinned. "Is it true?"

"What? Oh, yes, I expect so. Anyway, what does it matter? The tour is over. Come and meet the staff."

3

"Four guests booked for bed-and-breakfast," Sandy announced in a pleased voice. She and David were walking along the road, a black, single-lane ribbon between peat bogs. It was a warm afternoon, with clear skies overhead but clouds piling up in the west.

"Oh? Which ones?"

"The American couple, of course. You must remember them, or *Mrs.* Morrison anyway."

"I remember," David grinned. "She rather overshadows her husband, doesn't she?"

"She certainly does. The other two are Captain Moss, the retired Navy man, and that man with all the camera gear, Mr. Stevens. I forget his first name."

"I know who you mean." David dismissed those people with a gesture. "I'm glad you're getting some business at the castle, but right now I'm more interested in catching up on what's happened in the last couple of years. Wasn't that Aulay MacLure I saw playing his pipes just before the tour started? Has he been here the whole time?"

"Aulay was the last Laird's piper, butler and general manager of the castle, as you know. But he was on holiday visiting friends in Yorkshire when Ramshaw was caught and sent to prison."

"Did he have any idea what Ramshaw was up to?"

"Och, no. He and his wife expected to be back on the job in four weeks, so it was a big shock to them when they heard what happened. Of course, they had their pensions so they got by all right. They came back to Lewis and were living in the village until Mrs. MacLure died about six months ago. Then when the National Trust took over the castle, Aulay jumped at the chance to manage it. It was like getting his old job back."

"He must be pretty happy," David commented. "He sure looked it this morning. Now tell me some more about the ghost you mentioned on the telephone."

"Oh, that. There's not much to tell. See that house over there?" She pointed to the only house in sight, a stone cottage with obviously thick walls, tiny windows, and an ugly, corrugated iron roof. "Willie Meenie Craig lives there. She's the one who can tell you more about it."

"*What* did you call her?"

Sandy laughed. "Her name is really Williamina, but everyone calls her Willie Meenie. She lives alone except for a few sheep, some chickens and a cow. She's the only person who lives in sight of the castle."

She led David off the road along a path between wet grass and stacked peat to where the ground firmed and the house stood.

"This is what is known as a modernized black house."

"A black house?" queried David. The house was whitewashed to a dazzling brilliance.

"Yes," Sandy confirmed. "Originally there was no chimney, just a hole in the thatched roof for the smoke to escape, and the peat smoke blackened everything inside. These are the original walls and windows, but now there's a proper chimney and a new roof, and — " She stopped suddenly, almost at the door, frowning.

"Look at that," she whispered, pointing. A sprig of rowan in the shape of a cross hung above the door.

"Mountain ash," said David, giving it the Canadian name. "Just a decoration, isn't it?"

Sandy shook her auburn curls. "No, there's more to it than that. Rowan — that's what we call it — is a safeguard against the fairies, especially in the form of a cross."

"Against the *fairies!*" David looked at her in disbelief.

"Yes. Shh, I'll explain later," she promised as they heard movement inside and the door opened. A little woman with white hair and piercing black eyes stood there.

"Why, Sandy MacLeod! What a surprise." Her face glowed with pleasure. *"Ciamar a tha, mo ghaoil."*

"Tha ga math, Willie. I'm fine, thank you. This is my friend from Canada, David McCrimmon."

"Ah, young man, welcome to my home. Come away in, both of you. You'll just be in time for a *strupach*." She led the way in to where a kettle steamed on a peat fire. "Set you down there at the table and help yourselves to scones and jam. I was just about to have a bite myself."

It was a small room with handmade furniture and cupboards with sagging doors, but it was warm and cheerful with the sweet smell of burning peat.

Willie poured out the tea from an immense pot. "Help yourselves now," she urged. "Fill your baggies. There's plenty more scones, and I have a fresh batch of shortbread. You'd think I knew you were coming, wouldn't you?"

Sandy and David happily did as they were told, and the *strupach* disappeared amazingly fast. But after a few minutes Sandy brought up the reason for their visit. "David and I would like to hear about the ghost at the castle, Willie. You've seen it, haven't you?"

"Oh, aye. But I'm the only one, so no one pays much heed. And whether it was a ghost or not, I don't know. What I do know is that there was a light from one of the narrow windows at the top of the old tower."

"The *old* tower? You mean in the ruins?"

"Aye, that's the one. I saw it when I was out one night to see what was disturbing my chickens. Right plain, it was."

"What kind of light? A steady one, or flickering like a flame?"

"Not a flame, no, nor like an electric torch either. Just a light — a ghostly light. I saw it once in the tower, then once moving about among the ruins at the base. It moved slowly and — and *evenly*. As if it were moving itself, gliding, not being carried. Two nights I saw it, plain as plain."

"When was this?"

"Oh, a month ago. Six weeks. When the castle was still deserted."

"And not since? Sounds like someone just looking around — a tramp wanting a place to sleep maybe."

But both Willie Meenie and Sandy shook their heads. "Not in the tower, David," Sandy reminded him. "There's no way up into there except through the bars of the old iron yett, and no one's that thin. No person could have been up there. Did you see anything else, Willie?"

"Aye, a light from the new tower as well, and smoke from the chimney."

"But that was before anyone was using the castle. It should have been locked up."

"That's what people tell me," Willie agreed. "But I know what I saw. And ghosts don't need keys."

"No, I suppose not. Does that rowan cross above your door have anything to do with the ghost?"

"Och, no," said the old lady roundly. "That's a protection against the fairies."

"But it's new, isn't it? Why? Do you believe in fairies all of a sudden?"

"No, lassie, I don't believe *in* anything or anyone except God. To believe in means to trust, and I trust no one but God who has never let me down. Now if you are asking me if I believe the fairies exist, that's a different matter. Maybe I do, maybe I don't. But I'm not taking any chances."

"I don't understand," said David. "I thought fairies were imaginary little creatures who lived under toadstools and played and sang and never hurt anything. They're not something you need to be protected from."

"Highland fairies are different," Sandy told him. "They're little creatures, certainly, who dress in green and live underground and keep to themselves mostly, but if they're disturbed or crossed they can be very mean to humans. They can carry you off to their lands and you'll never be seen again."

"Aye," said Willie vaguely, "there are many tales. They love music, fairies do. I ken of a fiddler who was carried off to fairyland to play for a dance. So as not to offend them he played, as he thought, all night, and in the morning they let him go. But he found that in that one night ten years had passed. His children had grown up and his wife believed he had deserted her and the family."

"But those are old tales," said Sandy. "I know some people still have the old superstitions —"

"Sandy," interposed Willie, "there is nothing in the Book that speaks against the existence of *daoine sith* — the fairies. Aye, the Bible tells us there is a spirit world all around us and sometimes those spirits invade our human life. Call them fairies or kelpies or glaistigs or ghosts, there's plenty of things that cannot be explained by science, yet are true. You know what a *sithean* is?"

"Yes. A fairy knoll, where the fairies are supposed to live."

"Aye, and did you know there's a *sithean* on top of the headland behind the castle? I've known it was there for years, of course. There are old tales of strange happenings over the years, but as you say they are *old* tales and I paid them little heed. But recently I have heard the fairy music."

Two pairs of startled eyes turned to her as the old lady paused.

"It's music like I never heard before . . ." Her black eyes were shining, looking off into the

27

distance, somewhere far beyond the four walls. "No real tune to it, but the sound of a thousand tunes together in harmony, rising and falling, unearthly, beautiful. Oh, I can't describe it."

"And this was at the *sithean?*"

"Aye. I hadn't been that way in years, but I was out one fine day to check my flocks and I wandered there without thinking."

"And after that you put the rowan cross above your door."

"Aye, just in case. The cross of our Lord has power over all evil. And for all their beautiful music, the wee folk can be evil."

For a long moment there was silence in the room. David was uneasy, aware that these superstitions were very real to the old woman. And he thought Sandy wasn't totally sceptical either. Of course, she was a Highlander too. And so was he, ancestrally. And there *are* many strange happenings that science has as yet been unable to explain . . .

It was Willie who broke the silence. "You young people will not be paying any mind to an old woman and her imagination. That's fine. We all have our own beliefs and we're all in God's hands. But I saw the lights and the smoke, and I heard the music. Make of it what you will."

§　　§　　§

"Well, what do you think?" They were walking back along the road when David broke the silence again.

"As far as the *sithean* is concerned, she's talking about a cairn at the top of the hill, a megalithic cairn."

"A mega-what's-it cairn?"

"Megalithic. It's an ancient stone tomb, probably three or four thousand years old. They're fairly common throughout the Highlands. We'll go up and take a look at it some time, if you like. I expect the 'music' she heard was just the wind whistling through the stones and her imagination adding to it. But the lights must have been more than imagination. She must have seen something, and I'd like to know what it was. I doubt if the old Laird's wife has revived after all these years."

"Do you believe in — No, let me rephrase that. Do you believe ghosts exist?"

"Like Willie, I don't know. There's no doubt something apparitions, if you like — have appeared from time to time. I don't believe they're the restless souls of the dead, but I don't know a better explanation either. In this case though, I think we might be able to find a rational explanation for Willie's 'ghosts' with a little detective work."

"Great. I guess the logical place to start would be in the old part of the castle."

"Yes," agreed Sandy. "If there *was* a light in the old tower and it *wasn't* a ghost, I'd very much like to know how it got there. But we'll have to be careful. We're not even supposed to go into the old ruins because of the danger of falling stones."

David scoffed at that. "Those ruins have been the way they are for a hundred years. Why should they start to come apart now? I think the warning signs are just to protect the National Trust in case someone falls and breaks a leg or something."

"Probably. All the same, we don't want anyone to know what we're up to, right? We'll still have to be careful."

"That's true. And it might be difficult with guests here. We'll just have to wait for a good opportunity."

"Speaking of guests, we'd better be getting back to the castle now. I'm supposed to be available to answer any questions they may have at tea time."

4

A peat fire was burning in the lounge when Sandy and David reached the castle, and the four bed-and-breakfast guests were all there. Wally Morrison and his wife Irene were on a deep leather chester-field, Captain Moss was in a recliner behind a newspaper, and Timothy Stevens was adjusting a complicated camera for a flash shot. He looked up and smiled.

"Ah, our guide! Come join us for a cuppa."

"Thank you. You're Mr. Stevens, aren't you? Have you been getting any good pictures?"

"I hope so. Of course, I won't know until I've had them developed. This is a new hobby with me. Will you pose for me, Miss — Sandy, isn't it? A pretty girl beside old ruins — that's always a good picture. A classic. Contrast and all that."

"I do hope you'll let us have some of your pictures," interrupted Mrs. Morrison. "We just have a little disc camera, and of course we didn't know we'd find a real *Morrison* castle."

"Your pictures will likely be just as good as mine," said Stevens, modestly. "But if you leave me your address, I'll certainly send you some. How about you, Captain Moss? I haven't seen you taking any pictures."

The Captain folded the corner of his paper down and looked at them all from startlingly green eyes. "No, I don't go in for photography. I've been all around the world in the service and never took a picture in my life. No need to. I keep it all up here." He tapped his forehead. Then his eyes lit on David questioningly.

"Oh, sorry," said Sandy, catching the look. "This is David McCrimmon, everybody. He's from Canada, but he's on our staff here for the summer."

The ex-Naval officer acknowledged the introduction with a nod. Stevens did so by snapping David's picture. Wally Morrison struggled up from the deep settee to offer his hand.

"You must like it in Lewis to have come back again," he commented.

Before David could reply, Irene caught his other hand in hers. "Why, we're neighbours," she cried. "Wally and I are from Ohio. Toledo, actually. That's just across the border from Toronto, isn't it?"

David grinned and shook his head. "There are other cities and towns in Canada besides Toronto, you know. I'm from Woodstock, Ontario."

"Woodstock?" She frowned. "Never heard of it. Never mind, we're neighbours anyway. I've been to Toronto. Isn't this the cutest place?" She waved her hand to encompass the whole area. "Imagine, a Morrison castle! We're Morrisons, did you know? And we have a darling room. Imagine staying overnight in a real castle. And now they're going to serve us tea and cakes! Can you join us? Or doesn't the staff mix with the guests?"

Sandy laughed. "Thanks, we'd be delighted, if you'll have us. Have you had a chance to look around for yourselves?"

"Yes, we have." Timothy Stevens put his camera down. "And I learned about something you didn't mention in your tour — the ghost."

"But I told you that story," protested Sandy.

"The original story, yes," conceded the other. "But you didn't tell us that the ghost has reappeared recently."

David was aware of sudden silence, sudden tension in the atmosphere. Or was it just his imagination? He glanced around, puzzled. Everyone seemed to be giving Sandy the same expectant look.

She seemed a little taken aback. "Who told you that?" she asked.

"A man I met in the garden. The caretaker, I suppose. Is there any truth in it?"

"There have been rumours," she admitted. "A light was seen moving about, back when the castle was still empty. It was probably a hobo, of course, but a ghost makes a much better story."

"It certainly does," said Wally Morrison. "You should exploit it, you know. Why, when we have ghosts back in the States — "

"We make the most of them," broke in his wife, overpowering him. "And maybe embellish them a little if need be. But this is a natural place for a ghost. Where was it seen?"

"Among the old ruins," said Sandy. "Up in the old stair tower, for instance."

There was a sudden sound, like the sharp intake of a breath. David heard it, or thought he did. But no one appeared to be anything more than interested.

"And that's out of bounds, isn't it?" Timothy Stevens sounded disappointed. "I don't know why it should be. Those walls look pretty solid to me."

"When the Trust has the time and the money, the ruins will be strengthened so they don't deteriorate any further," said Sandy. "Until then, yes, they're out of bounds."

"There are ghost stories all over the world," observed the Captain dryly, "and they're all poppycock. Just imagination gone wild."

"Oh, don't say that," protested Irene. "You service men are too practical. You miss all the fun in life. Wait till I get home. I'll tell everyone we stayed in a Morrison castle — a *haunted* castle."

She broke off as the door opened and a

woman entered, carrying a tray laden with goodies.

"Tea time," she announced cheerfully. "This is tea and an extra pot of hot water, just off the boil. This is coffee, for anyone who prefers that. If there's anything else you would like, just come through and knock on the door to your left. Oh, Sandy, you're here. Good. And David too. Mr. MacLure is looking for you both. He's in the kitchen."

"Thank you, Mrs. McAllister." Sandy and David got up to go.

"Do come back," Irene invited. She had risen to take on the task of pouring the tea. "We want to hear more about the ghost."

"I don't think there's any more to tell," said Sandy, "but we will come back when we can."

§　　　§　　　§

Aulay MacLure was sitting at the kitchen table with a cup of tea in his hand. He looked worried about something, David thought.

"Good evening, Mr. MacLure. Mrs. McAllister said you wanted to see us?"

"Yes. I thought you should hear this. It was on the news half an hour ago." He looked at them oddly for a moment. "It's about Ramshaw — er, the former Laird. You know who I mean."

"Of course," said Sandy. "The man who's in prison. He may not be Ramshaw any more, technically speaking, but he'll always be Ramshaw to us, won't he, Davie? What about him?"

"He's not in prison any longer. He's escaped."

"Oh!" Sandy and David exchanged startled glances. "When did it happen?"

"Several days ago, apparently. The story just leaked out today. I expect the authorities were keeping it quiet, hoping to catch him and then make it public. But they haven't managed to find him. Not yet."

"So," muttered David, digesting the news, "he's free again. Did they say how he managed it?"

"A pretty daring escape, by all accounts. A helicopter suddenly came in over the prison wall and lowered a rope while the inmates were in the exercise yard. Ramshaw was waiting for it. It was all well planned."

David whistled. "Scary, isn't it, that underworld gangs can get away with that sort of thing? So his friends weren't all lost when his submarine was crushed. Thank God that bacillus was destroyed, at any rate. Or was it? Could it be —?"

Sandy shook her head. "No, it was. Well, I guess I don't really know for sure. I took it for granted that it was destroyed, but I don't *know*."

"What was all that about anyway?" asked the old man. "I never did hear a full explanation."

"It was a germ that spread a form of anthrax fatal to humans as well as cattle. I guess lots of that kind of stuff has been invented, or discovered, or whatever you do to produce something that can kill us all off in case the bomb doesn't do the job thoroughly. Germ warfare, they call it.

"I don't know who developed this particular germ, but Intelligence got wind of it and confiscated it. Ramshaw was in Intelligence at the time. He got away with some of the germ and was about to peddle it to terrorists for goodness knows how much money, but he was caught in the nick of time."

Aulay nodded. "Thanks largely to you two, I understand."

"Yes, we helped identify the island he was using as a base and then held him there until the Navy arrived to arrest him. And now he's loose again." David glanced at Sandy. "I'm sure he doesn't think too kindly of you and me, Sandy."

"To put it mildly," she agreed. "But we've nothing to worry about. This is the last place he would think of coming."

"That's right," nodded Aulay. "He'll be out of the country and far away by now." But his tone lacked conviction. Aulay MacLure was worried.

5

The Morrisons of Ramshaw. David picked up the book Sandy had given him, switched on the bedside light, and settled back to read. He skimmed through the pages, pausing to read parts that caught his attention.

There was a chapter about the fatal fall, the sealing off of the tower by the broken-hearted Laird, and the subsequent appearance of the ghost that he read with interest. The ghost had appeared a number of times over a period of more than a hundred years, but had not been seen since the Fletchers took over the castle.

Too bad, thought David sceptically, that someone with more imagination hadn't bought the place. In that case the ghost might have continued to appear.

Another chapter that caught his eye dealt with a siege of the castle by the MacKenzies. That story was highlighted by the unexplained escape of the Morrison leader from Ramshaw Castle. When the fortress surrendered to its enemies, the Laird had disappeared. The claim that he had not been in the castle at all was not believed by the invaders, but they were unable to find him. Two days later he turned up with a force of allies and recaptured the castle for the Morrisons.

David lowered the book thoughtfully. The answer was obvious — a secret passage. He grinned. This was going to be fun. A ghost, and a secret passage to find.

Suddenly he froze. A sound from his window, a scraping like claws on glass, chilled his blood. And he could hear movement in the darkness outside. He switched off the light. In the utter darkness of the room, the window became a square of faint light with something moving against it.

He slipped off the bed and approached the window cautiously, apprehensive in spite of himself. Whatever it was had gone. He looked out. For a moment he could see nothing but a few stars between black clouds. Then a movement on the ground below caught his eye. He could see a dark figure. Sandy. She was standing there with a long slender branch in her hand.

David chuckled in relief. He waved, not sure if she could see him. A few minutes later, fully dressed and with a small penlight in his pocket, he slipped out the side door and joined her in the darkness below his window.

"You weren't asleep, were you?" she whispered. "I saw your light."

"No, I was reading about the castle. What's up?"

"Our ghost is back, I think. I saw a light among the ruins. Just a flash."

"In the tower again?"

"No, at the base. But no one's supposed to be there."

"*We're* not either," David pointed out, "but that's not going to stop us. Someone else might have the same idea we have." He looked across the courtyard to the gaunt ruins crouching in the darkness, the tower climbing black against the sky. "Want to take a look?"

She hesitated. "What I want is to find a way up into that tower, but we can't do that in the dark. We'll have to wait until daylight. Tomorrow after I'm off duty we'll —"

He caught her arm. "Look! There's something moving over there."

An obscure figure was moving out of the shadows and across the courtyard, which was faintly lit now by a million stars. David's hand tightened on Sandy's arm. "It's a man," he whispered. "Who —?" Then he recognized him.

"Good evening, Captain Moss. Beautiful night, isn't it?"

The other man stopped short. His light

flashed on, catching them full in the face, then was quickly doused.

"Sorry," he said, "you startled me. I didn't see you till you spoke. Yes, it's a grand night."

"I saw your light a few moments ago," said Sandy, "and wondered if the ghost had returned."

He laughed. "I thought of that myself," he admitted. "I was out taking a constitutional and remembered your story. Took a closer look at the old wall. I hope you won't give me away to the National Trust. Didn't see anyone though," he added regretfully. "No ghost, I mean. Just the fellow with the cameras. What's his name? Stevens?"

"Timothy Stevens. He's out here too?"

"Yes. Over in the corner of the quadrangle, trying to take a time exposure of the old tower. Hoping to catch the ghost on film too, I expect. Morrison is around as well. Have you seen him? He's having a smoke. I expect his wife won't let him light up in their room. Well, I'm off to bed. Good night."

"Heavens," muttered David, "the place is crawling with tourists, even in the middle of the night. Don't blame them though. It *is* a grand night. Let's take a stroll."

He caught her hand as they moved away from the castle wall and walked through the opening that led to the car park and the road beyond. "Did you know there's probably a secret passage here somewhere, leading out of the castle?"

"A secret passage? I don't — Oh, yes, you're thinking of the escape of the Laird at the time of the siege, aren't you? I'd forgotten about it. That's something else we can look for. Well, there's no hurry. We've got all summer."

The canopy overhead was alive now with shimmering stars, almost close enough to reach out and be gathered in by the handful. They left the car park and started down the road, into a world that showed not a glimmer of man-made light.

They had walked for several minutes in companionable silence when they became aware of a figure approaching.

"Holy smoke!" breathed David. "The ghost of Rob Roy. It must be!"

The figure was in full highland dress, from the hackle feather in his balmoral bonnet to the knee socks and walking shoes visible beneath his kilt. Long white hair reached to his shoulders, and a matching beard straggled halfway down his chest.

"Hello, young lovers." The voice was musical. The man couldn't be as old as the beard suggested.

"Why, it's Dugald MacGregor," said Sandy. "You're a long way from home, Dugald."

"Aye, so I am. But it's a grand night, and I'm walking to Stornoway. Now don't tell me how far away that is, or you'll make me tired before my time. Is that you yourself, Sandy MacLeod?"

"Aye, it is. And this is David McCrimmon from Canada. David thought you were the ghost of Rob Roy. He wasn't far wrong, was he?"

"No, Rob Roy was a MacGregor and so am I. But if it's ghosts you're looking for, I just saw the ghost of that poor lass who was murdered in yon old tower of the castle."

"You saw the ghost? You're sure?"

"Och, no, I'm no' sure at all. You can't be sure of a thing when you're blazoomed, and it's a week now that I've been so."

"When you're what?" wondered David.

"Blazoomed." For explanation Dugald took a flask from his sporran, removed the cap, and tilted his head back for a long drink.

"I'd offer you some," he apologized as he replaced the cap with exaggerated care, "but you're better off without it. And there's not much left anyway."

Sandy had turned and was staring back at the castle. "You say you saw the ghost. Do you mean a light? And whereabouts? On the ground?"

"Aye, a light. But not on the ground. It was in the tower, near the top."

"Why didn't we see it?"

"Because you had your backs to it," he answered logically. "And if 'twas in the tower it could only be seen from out here. All the arrow slits and gun loops in the tower face outwards, and there's nary an opening else."

"How do you know that?"

"I've looked," said Dugald candidly. "Willie Meenie told me about the light. If I'd seen it myself I would have thought nothing of it, but Willie's never been blazoomed in her life. So I explored the castle, but I could find naught amiss. I thought she must have been dreaming. But now I've seen the light in the tower myself. And no human can get into the tower." His words were slurred just a little, the only indication that the whiskey had any effect on him.

"You said the lady was murdered," persisted Sandy. "Why? Any account I ever read said she fell by accident."

"Then the accounts you read were wrong. Ghosts only appear in the case of a violent death."

"I would have thought falling twenty metres would be violent enough," David remarked dryly.

"No, no, she was murdered. Pushed off the tower by her husband. The Laird was seeing another lady, you understand. His wife kicked up a fuss, so he did her in. Pushed her off the tower, then closed it off in a great show of grief. That's it."

"Wherever did you get that story?"

"Made it up," Dugald chuckled. "But I'll wager it's close to the truth all the same. She didn't fall, she was pushed, and that's why she's haunting the place."

"But the only thing anyone ever sees is a light, isn't it? No spooky figure vanishing through solid walls or anything like that?"

"Aye, that's true. Even *I* only saw a light, and I'm blazoomed — should see all kinds of things in my condition. But never mind. You'll be acting as guide to all these tourists, Sandy? You be sure they're told the truth about the ghost. The lady was pushed, mark my words." Dugald paused dramatically, then continued in a prosaic tone. "Time to be off now. Hope to reach Stornoway by daylight. *Oidhche mhath*."

They watched him go, an odd shape blending with the darkness.

"Who *is* he?" demanded David.

"A local character. He used to teach school until the drink took hold of him. Now he poses for tourists. No one knows what he lives on besides."

"Is he right about there being no windows in the tower?"

"Yes, he is. I hadn't thought about it, but of course all the arrow slits would be facing outwards. The Morrisons obviously wouldn't expect a rebellion from within. Any light shining inside the tower could never be seen from the castle grounds."

She stopped. Dugald had turned and was coming back to them. David noticed now that his step was just a little unsteady.

"Pardon me," he said as he reached them, "but what did you say the young man's name is?"

"David McCrimmon."

"Aye, so I thought. So you'll be the pair

responsible for putting Ramshaw behind bars."

"Yes," said Sandy, "more or less."

"Then I should be angry with you. You dried up my chief source of income."

"Oh? We're sorry about that. I didn't know you worked for him."

"Worked?" Dugald gave a peculiar little laugh. "He had another word for it. You see, I knew just a little too much about him."

"Did you know," enquired David, "that he recently escaped from prison?"

"Escaped!" It was hard to tell just what was behind the exclamaton. Surprise, definitely, but something else too. Apprehension somehow mixed with anticipation? "So, he has escaped. You will both be perhaps a wee bit anxious until he has been caught."

Sandy laughed. "I'm sure he doesn't remember us fondly, but I don't think he'll risk his neck and come here just for revenge."

"Not *just* for revenge, no. But maybe — aye, maybe you would be well advised to keep a weather eye out."

"Whatever for?"

"Och, never you mind. Pay no attention to me, I'm blazoomed, remember? As I said before, *oidhche mhath.*" He wheeled abruptly and left them.

They stared after him for a moment. "That's crazy," Sandy commented. "Why in the world would Ramshaw come back here?"

But David was thinking of something else. "Well, now you know how Dugald made his money. Blackmail. At least I think that's what he was hinting at."

"Blackmail? Dugald? That's hard to believe. And yet . . ." She caught David's hand. "Come on, let's go back."

They reached the castle and slipped through the opening back into the courtyard. They were crossing the square in silence, watched by myriad stars, when suddenly Sandy stopped and clutched David's arm.

"Did you hear that?"

"What? No. What was it?"

"Something over that way. A — a moan, I think. Do ghosts moan?"

"Probably." He held her hand tightly. He could hear nothing.

"If I was blazoomed," whispered Sandy, with a shaky laugh, "I would think nothing of it. But I'm sure I heard something."

"A cat," hazarded David. "A sheep from the moors maybe. Wait a minute! I have a penlight in my pocket. Want to check it out?"

"Yes, I think we should."

With the tiny light picking out a path, they again crossed the quadrangle, eyes searching the deep shadows below the ruins. Near the base of the tower they stopped.

"I don't see anything," whispered Sandy. "Let's try again, closer to the wall."

The light moved over the crumbling walls that had once been outer defences, wavered over mounds of stone that outlined long-vanished stables, and moved towards the far corner. Suddenly it faltered, stopped, swung back.

"There. There's something behind those stones." David had a sinking feeling in the pit of his stomach.

Sandy brushed past him. "Come on, someone's hurt." She snatched the light from him and shone it at her feet. A man with a great gash on his head and a blood-covered face lay in front of her.

"Oh, my Lord! David, it's Aulay MacLure. He's badly hurt. What in the world —? Run and get help, Davie. Get Mrs. McAllister, and call an ambulance. I'll stay with him and do what I can."

David turned and ran. He remembered all too vividly his last visit to Scotland, when he had found a man lying at the foot of a cliff. *That*, it turned out, had been murder. But this was an accident. In the tiny beam of light, he had seen a stone lying beside Aulay's head with blood on it. A stone from the crumbling wall.

6

"I guess I was wrong. I thought those walls were safe." Sandy sat miserably on her bed, tears in her eyes, her hand holding tightly to David's.

"Was he still alive," asked David gently, "when they took him away?"

"Yes, just. They didn't expect him to last to the hospital." There was a catch in her voice. "He didn't even know I was wiping his face. He was mumbling something, but it made no sense."

"What was it?"

"Part of it sounded like 'Ramshaw's here,' but there was a lot more that I couldn't make out. He must have been hallucinating."

David nodded. "He must have been. Ramshaw obviously isn't here. This is the last place he would come. But I do think Ramshaw's escape was worrying Aulay for some reason."

Why? David wondered. And what was the old man doing out among the ruins in the dead of night? Did it have anything to do with the ghost? He started to speak, then stopped. Sandy was too distraught to think about such things. They would have to wait.

But hours later the same questions were still bothering him. The police had decided after a whole day's investigation that Aulay had been involved in an accident. But David was not satisfied.

"I can't help thinking," he said to Sandy, "that Aulay was murdered."

Sandy sighed and shook her head. "I'm afraid you're letting our past adventures influence your thinking, David."

"Maybe," he conceded. "I know the police think it was an accident, but still . . . " He stared out the window into the courtyard. In the waning light he could see a policeman removing the yellow rope that had cordoned off the gaunt ruins all day.

"I just find it hard to believe that, for the first time in goodness knows how long, a stone should fall from that wall just at the moment Aulay was passing below."

"I know," said Sandy sadly. "And the police know too, but they've found absolutely no motive for murder. There's no reason why anyone would want to do away with that harmless old man. He had no enemies, no bank account, nothing."

"But you have to admit there's something strange going on here. What about the so-called ghost?"

"No one else is making anything of that,"

Sandy pointed out. "It's just another story that will attract tourists. We really should let it ride, like everyone else."

David looked at her keenly. "But we're not going to, are we?"

Sandy hesitated, then shook her head. "No, we aren't. But I don't see how it could have had anything to do with Aulay's death." She joined him at the window.

"All right, let's suppose, for argument's sake, that he *was* murdered. We keep coming back to the same question that stumped the police — why?"

David thought for a moment. "Why was he out in the ruins at that time of night anyway? Did he think he saw the ghost light? No, he couldn't have, at least not from the castle grounds. Your friend Dugald showed us that.

"And yet he was out there of his own free will. He wasn't clubbed somewhere else and dragged there to make it look like an accident. The police confirm that. For some reason he was there, and someone took the opportunity and killed him. But what was the reason? He *must* have seen someone or something. Something that shouldn't have been there. And the ghost is what keeps coming back to mind."

Sandy's hand closed suddenly on David's arm. She was looking down on the familiar scene, but she didn't seem to be aware of it. She turned to look at him, wide-eyed.

"Davie," she said, "suppose Aulay *was* the ghost."

"I beg your pardon?"

She shook her head, as if to clear it. "I know it sounds stupid. It's just an idea. Willie said she saw a light in the new tower as well as in the ruins, and smoke from the chimney. That could have been Aulay. I wouldn't be surprised if he kept a key to the castle when Ramshaw was imprisoned. I don't mean intentionally, but maybe he just never got around to returning it, or he didn't know who to give it to. Anyway, if he had a key he could certainly have gotten in."

"But why would he want to?"

"I don't know, but there may have been some reason. He was here all the time Ramshaw was leading a double life, remember. Maybe he recalled something, or was looking for something. I don't really know what I mean," she ended, lamely.

"Neither do I," said David. "But there may be something to your idea. Aulay was worried when he heard that Ramshaw had escaped. Didn't you think so?"

"Yes. And it must have been preying on his mind for him to have said what he did with his dying breath."

"Did you tell the police about that?" David asked.

Sandy was startled. "No, I never thought.

But it didn't mean anything anyway, except that he was delirious."

"Probably, but suppose it was true. Suppose Ramshaw *was* here, hiding out till the heat's off. If Aulay saw him and had to be silenced, that would be a motive for murder."

"It would be, but Ramshaw's not here. Where would he be hiding?"

"How about in the old tower? Either that light was a genuine ghost or *someone* has found a way into the tower. And who more likely than Ramshaw? He lived here all his life, didn't he?"

"Yes, but he couldn't have been the ghost. The light was seen long before his escape. Aulay lived here a long time too, though. I believe he worked for Ramshaw's father and was here ever since. And he was a lot more interested in the old place than Ramshaw ever was."

David nodded, then shrugged. "We're only guessing," he said. "And that's all we can do till we have a chance to explore those ruins. Who knows? We may be making a lot out of nothing. Maybe the original ghost really is back and Aulay's death *was* just an accident."

Sandy nodded slowly. "Perhaps. I'd like to be able to believe that." She broke off at the sound of a knock on the door. "Come in," she called.

Mrs. McAllister opened the door. "I'm serving our bed-and-breakfast guests a late tea in the lounge. Would you like to join them?"

"Oh, yes, thanks. They're still here then?"

"Aye, just for the night. They offered to leave this morning, under the circumstances, but I assured them they would be no bother, and I would be glad of something to do. But it has been decided that the funeral service will be held in the castle — Aulay would have liked that — so I will have plenty to do tomorrow. They all took it quite well. They'll be leaving in the morning."

"If there's anything we can do to help you get ready for the service, please let us know. When will it be?"

"The day after tomorrow. Until then we'll be closed to the public. After that, I don't know. The Trust will have to appoint a replacement for Aulay, I suppose. And thank you, I appreciate your help. Perhaps after breakfast we can start."

§   §   §

The four guests were seated in the lounge before a peat fire. In spite of the cheerful blaze, they were in a sombre mood. The captain was reading a book. Timothy Stevens was pacing restlessly, looking at the paintings on the walls without much interest. Wally Morrison was staring moodily into the fire. His wife had a fat paperback on her lap, but she was not reading.

"Hello, Sandy. And David," she greeted them eagerly. "Isn't this terrible? So sad. That poor old man." There were tears in her eyes. "And to think I was feeling angry with you for not letting us go into those ruins. They look solid, I told myself.

They'll never fall. But I was wrong. Why do you suppose —? Isn't it odd that the old man was out there in the middle of the night?"

"It was hardly the middle of the night," said Captain Moss dryly. "I was there myself only a half hour or so before he was found, as Sandy and David are aware. And so was Mr. Stevens."

"That's right," nodded the camera enthusiast. "I was trying to get a time exposure of the ruins. I suppose we're lucky we weren't the ones to be killed, Captain."

"You certainly are," said Irene severely. "You ought to obey the rules. I don't suppose any of you saw the ghost?" she added hopefully.

The other two shook their heads. "No such luck. But maybe Mr. MacLure did. *Something* made him go over there."

"Of course!" She beamed with excitement. "It must have been the ghost. He saw it and went to investigate. That explains everything. And you found him, didn't you, Sandy? That must have been a terrible experience. What were *you* doing out at that time of night?"

"Irene!" objected her husband mildly. "I don't think that's any of our business."

"Maybe not, but I want to know anyway. You don't mind, do you, Sandy?"

"Och, no," grinned Sandy. "David and I had gone for a walk down the road. We were crossing the courtyard when we came back and heard a groan. That's when we found him."

Captain Moss had laid down his book and was looking at them with interest. "You say he groaned. Did he say anything? I don't suppose he mentioned the ghost?"

"No, he didn't say anything that made any sense —"

She broke off. The door had opened, but it was not Mrs. McAllister with the tea, as expected. Dugald MacGregor stood there. A moment of startled silence greeted his exotic appearance. Then Irene Morrison squealed with delight.

"Oh, look, Wally! At last, a real Scotsman. The only people we've seen in kilts so far have been pipers. We were beginning to think no one else ever wears kilts in Scotland any more. Oh my, you do look positively . . . historical!"

She's right too, thought David. He was not as ghostly as he had appeared in the darkness of the preceding night, but though his kilt and tweed jacket were neat, his hair and beard gave him a wild appearance that made him resemble something out of the history books. Two bright eyes and a red nose peered and jutted from a mass of white whiskers.

"Hello, Dugald." Sandy stepped forward. "Let me introduce you to our guests. This is Dugald MacGregor, Captain Moss, Timothy Stevens, and Mr. and Mrs. Wallace Morrison."

"MacGregor!" cried Irene. "I should have known. I always think that's such a — such a

Scotch name, don't you? Do you always wear kilts, Mr. MacGregor?"

"Not kilts, mistress, just one at a time. I wear a kilt." The hair beneath his nose broke open unexpectedly to reveal a mouth when he spoke. "It's the most comfortable and practical form of dress ever devised by man."

"And that — that thing in your sock. What do you call it? Mr. MacLure wore one too, but his had a precious stone in the top. A topaz, I think."

"A cairngorm, madam, not a topaz." Dugald withdrew the thing in question from his sock. Light winked from the polished blade. "It's a *sgian dhu*, which is Gaelic for black knife. Aulay's was strictly for show. This one has a stag horn handle. It is — practical."

He slipped the knife back into place and turned to Sandy. "The sad news of Aulay's death has reached me. Tell me what happened."

While Sandy told him, David noticed that Dugald's bright eyes were busy, and he seemed to be studying each of the guests in turn. He won't see much of interest, thought David unkindly. One was idly twisting a pen between his fingers, one was drumming his fingers on the arm of his chair, the third was packing tobacco into the bowl of his pipe in a manner that seemed oddly familiar to David. Irene was staring at Dugald in fascination. She broke the silence that followed Sandy's account of the discovery of the body.

"Timothy, where's your camera? I suppose

now that we have something worth snapping you've left it in your room. Mr. MacGregor, would you mind terribly if we posed together? Wouldn't I just love to show my friends back home a picture of me with a *real* MacGregor, in a *real* haunted castle! Oh, do say yes."

"My pleasure, my lady. I can spare a few minutes. But only if you let me pose with you all, and promise to send me a copy when you have it developed."

"I'll do better than that," offered Timothy. "I'll get my Polaroid, and we can have instant results."

Neither the Captain nor Wally Morrison were too anxious to participate in the picture taking, and Timothy wasn't eager to let anyone else handle his camera so that he could be included, but eventually everyone present had a photo of the group, including Dugald MacGregor in his flowing beard and Highland finery.

"Now," said Dugald at last, "You'll have to excuse me. I suppose the body has been removed?"

Sandy nodded. "It's at the funeral home. There are no immediate relatives, just neighbours and friends as mourners. You'll be able to see them tomorrow."

"Thank you." Dugald bowed gravely, bonnet in hand, to the others and turned away.

"Wasn't that exciting!" murmured Irene. "He looked so — so Highland, didn't he? And did you see the flask in his sporran? Whiskey, I'm sure of it."

"And he could hardly wait to get away so he could have a drink," said the Captain with a touch of sarcasm.

"Oh, that's unkind," protested Irene. "His nose is just weather-beaten. Don't you agree, Wally?"

"I wouldn't blame him if he did want a drink," muttered Wally. "He must get tired of tourists asking him for his picture if he goes around dressed like that all the time."

"Don't worry," grinned Sandy. "He enjoys it."

7

Some time later David picked up *The Morrisons of Ramshaw* once again and lay down on his bed to read. But a knock on the door startled him before he could even decide which chapter to look at next. A moment later Sandy slipped in, a look of great perplexity on her face.

"Sandy, what's up?"

"I don't know. I just had the strangest call from Dugald." She sat on the edge of the bed, her brows lowered in a worried frown.

"Why, what did he say?"

"He said, 'Sandy, you and the young lad had better be careful. Ramshaw's at the castle.'"

David sat up with a jerk, a prickly sensation running down his spine. "That's the same thing Aulay MacLure said! But what —? Did he actually *see* Ramshaw?"

"So he said, but he didn't say when or where."

"It had to be after he left us tonight,"

reasoned David. "Outside in the car park maybe. Didn't he tell you any more?"

"No. I told you it was a strange call. He told me Ramshaw was here and I asked what he meant. His answer was, 'When I heard about Aulay's death, I began to wonder if he'd been murdered. That's why I came to the castle tonight. And sure enough, I saw Ramshaw.'"

"Then he must have been expecting to see him." David was excited. "And he obviously thinks Ramshaw killed Aulay. What else did he say?"

"Nothing."

"What do you mean nothing? He can't have just left it at that."

"Yes, he did. That's the queer part. He had just finished saying 'I saw Ramshaw' when there was some kind of noise in the background. He didn't say another word, and for a minute I couldn't hear anything at all. Then he suddenly hung up, just like that."

"And that's all?"

"Yes. I waited a couple of minutes to see if he'd call back. I thought maybe we'd been cut off accidentally. Finally I tried to call him, but I got no answer."

"What kind of noise did you hear in the background?"

"Just a — a sort of muffled bump. It could have been anything. I didn't even worry about it until he — or someone — hung up like that."

"Or someone?" David swung off the bed, his

book dropping unheeded to the floor. He began to pace. "If there's someone else there —" He didn't complete the thought — the possibilities were too disturbing. "But he knows Ramshaw's an escaped convict. Why didn't he call the police?"

"Perhaps he called them first, then called to warn us since we were responsible for Ramshaw being in prison in the first place."

"Or perhaps he didn't call them at all. Maybe he's hoping to re-open his blackmail scheme. And that's a dangerous game. You don't fool around with a man like Ramshaw for very long. Are you sure he was calling from his house?"

"No, he didn't say so, but there are no call boxes between here and there. Do you think we should go there to make sure he's all right?"

"Can we? Where does he live?"

"This edge of the village. It won't take long by car."

"What car? Do you have one?"

"It's Uncle Rory's, but I have the use of it while he's at sea."

"Great! Let's go. Quietly so we don't disturb anyone. The others are probably in bed by now."

They slipped stealthily down the stairs and out the side door. A light still shone from one of the guest rooms, but otherwise they saw no sign of life.

"How in the world," objected David as they crossed the car park, "did Dugald see *anyone* in this darkness? Could he have been driving?

Maybe the headlights picked up someone."

"No, he doesn't own a car. He walks everywhere."

They stopped at the far side of the car park. Sandy opened the left-hand door of a Nova and motioned him in.

"No, no," muttered David, "you drive. I'm not used to driving on the left side of the road."

She giggled. "I intend to drive. This is the passenger's side. Come on."

She backed the car out and headed down the road. It was one of the single-track roads found here and there throughout the Highlands, well surfaced but with only infrequent lay-bys for passing. There was no traffic, but the probing headlights caught sheep wandering here, there and everywhere, including down the middle of the road. It took time for them to wander off and let the car pass, but that was a normal hazard on a Lewis road.

They drove for long minutes before a single light broke the unrelieved darkness. "That's the village up ahead," Sandy announced. "Dugald's house is right here."

"You could have fooled me. I don't see a thing."

"It's here all right, in total darkness. I'm not going to stop though. We'd better go on in case someone's watching. Then we'll park in the village and walk back. I hope you brought your torch."

"My flashlight? Yes. A decent-sized one this

time. We'll have to be careful how we use it though, just in case."

Just in case there's someone there who shouldn't be, he thought, but he didn't say it.

A few minutes later they studied the obscure shape of the house from the shelter of a peat stack. It was a tiny dwelling, much like that of Willie Meenie. There was no sign of life.

"Let's see if we can see anything through the windows," whispered Sandy.

They pressed their faces against the glass of the first window, but could see nothing inside. David risked a brief flash of light and shook his head.

"It's the kitchen. Other than that I can't see a darn thing."

The other windows proved to be no more enlightening.

"If there's anyone in there," whispered David, "he's asleep. Or hiding. Or unconscious." Or dead, he thought, but he didn't say that either. "Are you game to try the door?"

"No need to try it, it'll be open. I doubt if he ever locks it."

The door opened easily when they pushed it, but it creaked alarmingly. They froze, breathless. The only sound was the thudding of their hearts. Nothing happened. David caught Sandy's hand, then raised the flashlight and pressed the button.

The beam of light swept over an untidy living room with no one in it. Through a door off to one side a mirror reflected the light, startling them.

The bed inside was sloppily made up and had not been slept in. They found no one either there in the bedroom or in the kitchen. Except for the two of them, the house was empty.

Back in the living room, David found a switch and turned on the overhead light. "Now," he observed, looking around the room, "if we're any good at detecting, we should be able to find a clue that will tell us just what went on here tonight — if anything."

"Well," said Sandy after a moment, "there's a newspaper on the floor, but that fits in with the general disorder. Knowing Dugald, I would be suspicious if everything was neat and tidy. There's certainly nothing to suggest a — a struggle, or anything like that."

"But you didn't hear anything like a struggle, did you? Just a bump, you said. If his door was open, someone could easily have walked in and coshed him while he was talking. Where's the telephone?"

"Over there." Sandy pointed to a table beside the window. "By someone," she spoke slowly, "you must mean Ramshaw. Do you think he might have followed Dugald from the castle, then hit him on the head to prevent him from talking?"

David was on his knees examining the floor. "If Dugald really did see Ramshaw, I'd say that's a possibility. But there's no blood or anything here as far as I can see. Of course, we're not even sure he made the call from here."

"Oh, yes, we are," said Sandy, with a new note of excitement in her voice. "He must have been here. Look at this."

She held out a photograph, a polaroid shot of Dugald with the four castle guests. David whistled.

"That's one of the pictures taken tonight. Where was it?"

"Here beside the phone, face down."

David looked at it for a moment, then slipped it into his pocket. "So he *was* here. But he's gone now. Gone in the middle of a telephone call. Do you think we should call the police?"

"And tell them what?"

"Tell them what happened. Tell them first of all that Dugald claims Aulay MacLure was murdered."

Sandy shook her head. "He also claims the girl who fell from the tower hundreds of years ago was murdered, on no evidence whatever."

"Well, okay. But he believes he saw Ramshaw at the castle. And now he's missing."

"He isn't missing, he's just not at home. You don't know Dugald's reputation, Davie. He's 'blazoomed' most of the time, living in a fog, seeing things that aren't there. He admits it himself. Sometimes I almost wonder if he's faking it so people will discount him, laugh at him."

"That could very well be. And all the time he's doing the laughing while he quietly blackmails his victim."

"Yes. But regardless of that, no one will believe he saw anything. And the fact that he's not at home won't mean much either. He's one of the 'children of the mist' who wander here, there and everywhere. We met him walking to Stornoway in the middle of the night, remember? No, if our only witness is Dugald MacGregor, we might as well forget it. We'll have to have more than his word to go on if we want the police to listen to us."

"You mean — like a body."

She shivered. "Don't say that. We don't know he's dead. And we won't find out anything in the darkness tonight."

"No, that's for sure. Think we should come back tomorrow and look around?"

"If we have a chance after we help Mrs. McAllister prepare for the funeral, then yes. But I have another idea too. If Dugald is missing, the best way to find him may be to learn the truth about Ramshaw and the ghost. Let's get up first thing in the morning and have a look around those ruins before anyone else is up. There simply *must* be a way into that tower."

"Okay. But what do you mean by 'first thing'?"

"Daybreak," she answered firmly. "I have an alarm. I'll wake you."

8

The sign above the opening in the old wall read *Absolutely No Admittance*. Sandy and David ignored it and stepped through into the ruined wing of the castle. The ancient outer wall of the keep soared above them. Four rows of gaping windows and four huge fireplaces with richly carved mantles showed where floors, long since disintegrated, had once been. Inner partitions too had disappeared, but at one end, across a cobbled floor, stood the tower, round and solid, intact to the castellated top.

The doorway into the tower was sealed off by a great iron yett. The thick bars were only centimetres apart, their ends buried and secured into the walls forever.

"I see what you mean about this tower," David admitted when he and Sandy stood before the gate, awed. "You'd have to tear the walls down before you could get in there. And look how thick they are! Three metres, at least."

They tested the bars, one at a time, but not with any hope. As they had expected, all were solid, immoveable. They peered through them into the tower itself. The wall blocked off the view to the left. On the right, a spiral stair against the wall led upwards. It wound as high as they could see before their view was cut off by the thickness of the lintel.

"I don't understand," said David. "How did anyone get to the upper floors of this wing after the tower was closed off?"

"Oh, there was another stair at the far end. The first few steps are still there to show where it was. The tower stair did open to every floor, but the Laird ordered all the doors walled up when he closed the tower. You can still see where they were though."

They stood back to look up the inside wall of the tower. Sure enough, they could see the shape of a door on every floor, but each had been sealed off with a stone wall.

"There was once an opening onto the roof too," said Sandy. "There had to be, of course, for defence. But when the Laird sealed off the tower, he closed and locked that door and publicly threw the key into the sea. I don't know what it was made of. If it was just wood I suppose it would be possible to break into the tower that way. But first you'd have to get up there."

"Which," said David with a laugh, "is impossible without a very long ladder or the ability to climb walls like a fly." He stared at the impregnable walls, examining them as well as he could. "I give up," he said finally. "There's no way in there. It's beginning to look more and more as if the light was a ghost after all."

Sandy shook her head stubbornly. "There has to be a way in. If the light had acted more like a ghost is supposed to act, I might give in. But ghosts aren't just lights, they're — they're spectres, figures. Maybe you can see through them, but —" She broke off. David's attention had been caught by something on the floor almost at their feet. It was an iron grating.

"What's that? A sewer?"

"No," said Sandy, "it must be the bottle dungeon."

"What's a bottle dungeon? Some kind of wine cellar?"

Sandy laughed. "Hardly. It's a prison shaped like a bottle, a special prison for permanent captives, not ones being held for ransom. Have you got your flashlight?"

David nodded. He shone his light through the grating into a shaft perhaps a metre across.

"See," she said, "this is the neck of the bottle. It opens out into a larger room below, but this is the only entrance. Prisoners were dropped in and there was absolutely no way out. They were usually left to rot."

David whistled. "Nice people, these Morrisons."

"I hate to admit it," said Sandy, "but these

were common throughout Scotland, and probably the world. I don't think the Scots had any monopoly on cruelty. The MacLeods refined their bottle dungeon by drilling holes from it to the kitchen. That way the prisoners could smell the food without getting any. It drove them mad before they starved to death."

"Yuck!" David made a wry face. "And to think I'm associating with a MacLeod."

"Don't worry," chuckled Sandy, "I can think of other tortures to inflict on you if you ever become my prisoner."

"Oh?" David looked interested. "Such as?"

"I'm not telling. I wonder what our friend Irene Morrison would say if she saw this."

"That's easy." David grinned. "She'd remind us that she just married into the family, and besides, Wally's people came from the mainland." He poked tentatively at the grate. "Hey, this thing moves. I bet we could get down in there if we had a ladder."

"Would you *want* to?"

He looked at the tower, measuring the distance between it and the grate with his eye. "I can't see how big the bottom part of this bottle is," he said, "but it might almost reach under the stair tower. And if it does, you never know . . . "

Sandy's eyes lit up. "It's worth a try. Let's see if we can remove the grating."

It moved easily. As they pulled it back, Sandy noticed for the first time some scrape marks on the rounded tops of the cobblestones. "Look." She was suddenly whispering. "Someone else has moved this thing. And recently, I'd say."

David nodded in excitement. "Maybe we're onto something here. But whoever it was must have had a ladder if he actually went down into the dungeon. And we need one too."

"There's one out in the courtyard, I think. The police were using it to check the walls."

There was no sign of action around the lived-in part of the castle. They made sure of that before they slipped out through the forbidden doorway. A lightweight aluminum extension ladder was propped against the wall close to where they had found Aulay. They carried it back into the ruins and lowered the end into the neck of the bottle.

"You first," whispered Sandy. "I'll check again to make sure no one is coming."

She joined him a few minutes later at the foot of the ladder. "Somebody's awake," she reported. "I saw the curtains pulled back in one of the rooms upstairs, but I couldn't see who it was. They're not likely to come in here, but I think we should pull the grating back just in case."

"Good idea." He climbed up again and managed, with an effort, to replace the cover, then lowered the ladder and laid it on the floor, out of the line of vision of anyone who might look down into the dungeon.

"Now," he said, "let's see what we have here."

They were in a room some three metres square. The walls were solid stone, on three sides at least. David swung the light to the wall that he reckoned must be almost under the tower.

"Look at this, Sandy." There was suppressed excitement in his voice. "Some of these stones have been moved recently. See the marks in the floor? And there's no mortar around them. Give me a hand."

They worked their hands into the crevice above the upper of two large stones in the wall. It moved. They pulled hard until it finally fell with a thud at their feet. They caught their breath and stood silent, listening. But there was no other sound.

"Let's move the other one." The bottom stone moved easily, leaving an opening large enough to crawl through. David poked his head into the aperture and shone the light upwards. When he turned around he was grinning triumphantly.

"We've found it! The wall's hollow. Not only that, there's an iron ladder leading up into the tower. Look!"

She looked. When she turned back there was a quizzical look on her face. "I'm beginning to think Dugald was right. The Laird of Ramshaw who closed off the tower must have been a bit of a rascal. He did all that and yet he had his own secret entrance into it."

"What for?"

"I suppose so he could get up onto the roof. I

wonder if he used it to visit his lady friend some-times."

"I don't know," David grinned. "But more important now is the fact that we know how our 'ghost' got into the tower."

"That's right." Sandy was frowning. "But we still don't know why. You have the light. You'd better go ahead."

David crept again into the opening and climbed the vertical ladder, then shone the light down for Sandy to follow.

They found themselves on the main level, hidden by the thickness of the tower wall from the iron yett. The staircase spiralled up opposite them. Away up above they could see daylight.

They looked around. There was certainly nothing to see on that level. "All right," Sandy said, "onward and upward. There must have been something higher up to attract our ghostly friend."

At one time there must have been a ban-nister of sorts, but there was none now. David and Sandy kept close to the wall as they climbed the stone stairs. At each level they found a land-ing and a shallow alcove that had once been a doorway, as well as arrow slits and gun loops on the outer walls. But there was nothing else. They passed three such levels, and still the stair led upwards.

When they reached the next level they found that whatever kind of door had once sealed the tower off from the wing roof was no longer there. They exchanged an excited glance.

"This must be it," David declared. "Willie Meenie said she saw the light at the top of the tower. The ghost must have been up here."

"It certainly seems so," agreed Sandy. "The rest of the tower has nothing that would interest a ghost."

They stepped carefully out onto the parapet, high above the ground. It projected out over the walls, with apertures in the floor through which defenders, at one time, must have poured boiling oil on the attacking MacKenzies. Around the high ramparts were numerous narrow embrasures through which the Morrison men once fired on their foes.

Sandy and David explored thoroughly, eagerly, sure that they would find something. But finally they gave up. Here, as elsewhere, there was nothing. Nothing at all to explain why someone had been prowling the tower with a light.

9

Sandy sat leaning back against the rampart. "Well, that's it," she frowned. "We've solved the mystery of the tower, but I can't see that we're any further ahead."

David was still circling the tower, looking out over the countryside below. Away to the south, the purple hills of Harris loomed into the sky. To the west, a plume of smoke rose vertically from Willie Meenie's chimney. To the north, he looked across at the pile of stones that marked Willie's fairy cairn. Except for sheep, the countryside was empty. He moved to look inward over the castle itself, but Sandy checked him.

"Be careful," she warned. "People are up by now. They might see you."

"Not very likely," he denied, but he sat down beside her anyway. "You're right," he agreed after a moment. "We know how the ghost got up here now, but we still haven't found out why."

"I've been doing a lot of thinking," said Sandy. "I didn't get much sleep last night, but I came up with a few ideas. Want to hear them? Some of them are pretty wild."

"Better wild than nothing. And this is a great place to listen. Go ahead."

"Okay. Let's suppose it was Aulay MacLure who was in this tower with a light. He was an old man, so we can be sure he wasn't climbing around here just for the fun of it. Let's imagine ourselves in his place.

"Aulay has worked for Ramshaw for years, but suddenly his boss is arrested for smuggling. 'How can this be?' he asks himself. 'How could he be carrying on his nefarious schemes right under my nose, and me none the wiser?' Then he begins to remember certain happenings — strangers coming and going at odd hours, perhaps activities around these ruins. Before, if he thought about them at all, he put them down to the fact that Ramshaw was in Intelligence. But now he begins to wonder.

"Ramshaw was a smuggler. Could it be that he was hoarding some of his contraband goods here at the castle? And if so, was it possible there might still be some here, somewhere? So, after his wife's death, with nothing else to do, Aulay comes here in the dead of night to have a look for himself."

"That makes sense," said David eagerly. "And it explains why Ramshaw might come back here — to retrieve some of his ill-gotten goods and cash them in." Then his eagerness subsided. "If so, we're too late. There's nothing here now."

Sandy put her hand on his arm. "Wait a minute. There are three possibilities. First, there never was anything here."

"Then why would Ramshaw come back?"

"I don't know. Second, Aulay already found it and removed it."

"Or Ramshaw already found it."

"No. If so, why would he stay? And he was still here last night, according to Dugald."

"Okay. What's number three?"

"Third, whatever it is, it's *still* here."

"Hah! Where?"

"The only possibility I can come up with is down in the hollow wall. Remember, when we saw the ladder leading up here we were so excited that we didn't explore any deeper into the wall."

David thought for a moment, then nodded slowly.

"That's true," he conceded. "But it would have to be something pretty small."

"It doesn't have to be big to be valuable. Remember the Loon Lake necklace? That was pretty small, but it was worth three quarters of a million dollars."

"That's true. I was thinking more along the line of guns and the sort of thing Ramshaw used to peddle to terrorists. But he might have had something else hidden away to fall back on in case of emergency. Something the rest of his gang didn't even know about. Maybe that's why he left it here. Let's go down and take another look into that wall."

"No, wait a minute. I have one more idea. And this is the really wild one. How well did you know Ramshaw?"

David was surprised. "I wouldn't say I knew him well at all. Let's see. I talked to him for a few minutes on board the *Skerryvore* the first time I met him. Then he had us to dinner in the castle that one evening. But you were there too, so I wasn't paying much attention to anyone else." He grinned, remembering. "You wore a — a dress of some sort. I'd only seen you in jeans before that."

"It's Ramshaw we're talking about," she broke in, eyes twinkling. "Not me."

"Oh, yes. Well, I talked to him again for a while after dinner that night, along with Commander Stanley, but those are the only times I saw him, except for the day he was captured. You must have known him better than I did."

"No, I didn't. The only time I was ever in his company was that same night at dinner, and like you, I didn't pay much attention to him. And he left me right after dinner to go off with you." She hesitated. "Do you remember what he looked like?"

"Ramshaw? Oh, sure."

"Describe him."

"Well, he had a moustache — a squarish, military one. And hair that was dark with grey in it. I don't remember the colour of his eyes. Blue, I think. Medium height. Nothing really outstanding about him, about his features, I mean. But he gave me the impression of — of competence, I suppose."

She nodded slowly. "That's about right, as I remember. Have you still got that picture we found by Dugald's phone last night?"

He was mystified, but felt in his pocket. "Yes, here it is."

"Good. Let me see it." She held it so they could both look at it. "Now," she said, "do you see the Laird of Ramshaw in that picture?"

"What?" He looked at her incredulously. "Of course not. What are you talking about?"

"Just a minute, don't get excited. Suppose Ramshaw shaved off his moustache, dyed his hair, and altered his appearance as much as possible with make-up. *Could* he be one of the people in that picture?"

"You've got to be kidding!" Nevertheless, David looked at the picture with new interest.

"Dugald said he saw Ramshaw at the castle," Sandy persisted. "Where did he see him? Remember how dark it was last night. And he didn't have any time to look around outside. Judging by the time he telephoned me, he must have gone directly home. And where did we find this photo? Right by the telephone. He was looking at it when he was talking to me. *He* knew Ramshaw very well. I think he recognized him as one of the guests."

For a long moment David stared at the picture. Then he slowly shook his head. "Actually," he said, "I suppose with his moustache gone, hair dyed, and good use of make-up, he could be any one of these three. I think we can rule Irene Morrison out."

"Yes," agreed Sandy with a chuckle. "She's definitely *not* a man in disguise. Let's start with the hair. Captain Moss is dark, Timothy Stevens is fair. Both could be dye jobs. Wally Morrison's is kind of mouse-coloured and thin at the back."

"A dye and shave job," suggested David.

"Possible. Now, the eyes."

"Captain Moss is out," said David, definitely. "Whatever colour Ramshaw's eyes are, they are *not* as green as the Captain's. He has the greenest eyes I've ever seen."

"Have you never heard of contact lenses? *Coloured* contact lenses? We can't go by eye colour at all. Nor eye brows. They can be thinned or shaped. Faces can be made to look fatter — like Wally's — by storing something in the cheeks. And his little paunch could be fake too, of course. Captain Moss's beard certainly looks real. Do you think it could have grown that much since the escape?"

"Probably, it's fairly short. You know, Sandy, now that you mention it, there have been a couple of things that rang a bell somewhere in my subconscious. Something one of them said or did, or both. I just can't put my finger on it."

She looked at him keenly. "Try to remember. No, *don't* try. It will probably come to you more easily if you don't try too hard." She stopped suddenly, her hand reaching to touch his arm. "Davie, look! Who's that?"

A man was walking across the moor below. He had obviously come from the direction of the castle, and was warily crossing the peat hags. His movement was hampered by the fact that he mistrusted the ground. And not without reason, for it was soft after the spring rains. Pools of water sparkled in the sunlight here and there.

The man was carrying a satchel and seemed to have a definite objective in mind, but he had to change direction frequently in his search for solid footing.

"It's Wally Morrison!" exclaimed David. "Where in the world is he going?"

"It's certainly a strange place to choose for a morning stroll." Sandy was intrigued. "What do you suppose he has in that bag?"

David shook his head. "I haven't the faintest idea."

They watched in silence as the American continued his erratic journey. Soon it brought him to a stream that tumbled and sparkled down the slope below the cairn. At a spot where the stream widened into a small pool, he stopped and knelt down with the satchel in front of him. His bent back prevented them from seeing what he was doing. After a minute or two he stood and turned, satchel in hand.

David and Sandy stepped back quickly so they would not be seen if he should happen to look up at the top of the tower. They stared at each other.

"What in blazes?" David shook his head, bewildered. "He either put something in that creek or took something out."

"Burn," corrected Sandy absently.

"Burn? What do you mean 'burn'?"

"I mean we call a stream a burn, not a creek. You must be right about why he was there, but it doesn't make sense."

"Like a lot of other happenings around here," agreed David. "Well, it shouldn't be too difficult to solve *this* mystery. We can go out there and see what he was up to."

"Not if he was taking something out and hasn't left anything behind to give him away," pointed out Sandy. "Let's go down quickly and meet him 'accidentally' when he gets back. That way we might be able to see what he has in the bag."

They descended the steep stair as fast as caution permitted, then lowered themselves down into the dungeon. A few minutes later they were back on the floor of the ruined wing of the castle, the grating in place over the bottle neck.

"Now," said Sandy, "we'll have to return the

ladder, and there's a good chance we're going to be seen. I'm sure there will be people up and about by now. So we'd better act unconcerned."

"Nonchalant's the word," agreed David. "Let's go."

They each took one end of the ladder, and David led the way out of the ruins.

"Well, good morning! You two are at work early."

David's heart leapt into his mouth at the sudden voice. Timothy Stevens was standing there, camera in hand.

"Good morning. You startled me." Was Timothy looking suspiciously at the ladder? For a moment David was tempted to try to explain it away, then thought better of it. He and Sandy were, after all, members of the staff, and as such were certainly not answerable to the guests.

Timothy looked up at the warning notice overhead and grinned ruefully.

"You caught me in the act," he admitted. "I thought if I came out early enough I could get into the forbidden area without being seen. I know it's off limits, but you must admit this old part of the castle is very picturesque. Now that I'm here, do you suppose I could take a peek inside? I'd love to get a picture in there."

"That's up to you," said David. "The sign absolves the Trust of any responsibility. If a wall collapses on you, you won't be able to sue for damages."

"Right, I understand that. I'll take the

chance. Surely two accidents like that can't happen so close together." He turned to Sandy. "How about a guided tour?"

She hesitated, looking anxiously at David. He turned to look across the courtyard. There was no sign of the American yet.

"Of course," she agreed, "though there isn't much to tell. Davie, if you'll put the ladder away ..." And then intercept Wally Morrison, her eyes finished the sentence.

"Oh, I'll help you with that later," offered Timothy. "I'd like to get a picture of both of you. Do you mind?"

"I hardly think we're dressed for that."

"Nonsense. I'm not talking about portraits. The casual look is what I want — staff checking the walls for dangerous rock falls. I suppose that's what you were doing?"

David and Sandy ignored the question, but Timothy didn't notice. "At any rate, a pretty girl enhances any picture, as everyone knows."

"That lets me out then," said David quickly.

"No, no, you too. You'll help give the wall proportion. Why don't you both stand over there. That used to be a fireplace, I take it? With a coat of arms above it?"

"That's right. The Morrison crest."

Timothy took his time arranging them on either side of the ancient hearth, then finally snapped three shots.

"Now the tower." He looked up to the top and

whistled softly. "So that's where the lady fell. Yes, that would be fatal, no doubt about it. And you're sure there's no way in there any more?"

"The gate's right there," said Sandy. "You can see for yourself."

His path took him right over the grating which he stepped on without a second glance. He studied the gate for a moment, shook the bars as Sandy and David had done, then stepped back to photograph it.

"Interesting," he commented. "It certainly appears to be solid." His foot came down on the grating again, and this time he noticed. "What's down there?"

"A bottle dungeon," Sandy answered with forced casualness.

"Oh, one of those." Timothy was evidently familiar with bottle dungeons and not impressed. "Well, I suppose that will be all for just now. I do think I'll come back here for a day or two after the funeral though. The breakfasts are top-notch, and the location is ideal for touring."

"Oh?" Sandy was interested. "Do you think any of the others will be returning?"

"The Morrisons, definitely. We've got rooms in the same house in Callanish for tonight. Irene has bought a film for me to use so she'll be sure to have pictures of a 'real haunted castle.' Don't know about the Captain. I believe he's going to Stornoway. Now, can I help you with that ladder?"

"Oh, no thanks," said David. "We'll manage, no problem." He had just seen Wally Morrison entering the side door, satchel in hand. There was no hurry now.

10

After breakfast, Sandy and David spent a busy day tidying the house and grounds, helping prepare a lunch for the funeral guests who would return to the castle after the interment, and going in to town for supplies. On the return trip they stopped at the cemetery as requested to make sure the grave had been dug.

David was surprised by the request. "Isn't this the responsibility of the funeral director?"

They had parked Sandy's car at the side of the road and were opening the gate to the cemetery.

"Of course it is," agreed Sandy, "but Mr. Mac-Donald is not very reliable. He has been known to forget things. And to make matters worse, he sometimes employs Dugald MacGregor to help him. Between the two of them anything can happen."

"It would be a relief to know that Dugald

helped him this time," David said. "If so, my theory that he was bashed over the head while talking to you on the phone would be all wrong."

Sandy nodded. "I hope it's all wrong, but if so . . ." If so, she was thinking, why had Dugald broken off his conversation? Why had he not called back or answered the phone when she returned the call? No amount of drink would explain those questions, not in the case of Dugald MacGregor, whose capacity for booze was legendary.

David was interested in the names and dates on the tombstones, many of them well over two hundred years old. There were MacKenzies and MacLeods and, of course, MacDonalds in profusion. There were also MacAulays and MacIvors and Nicolsons and others.

He had stopped and knelt down before one stone, trying to decipher the date, when something in the grass nearby caught his eye. He picked it up.

"Hey, Sandy!" She had gone on ahead. "Look at this."

She came back and took it from him.

"Is that what I think it is?" he asked.

She nodded, frowning. "It's Dugald's *sgian dhu*." She held it so he could see the hilt. "It's a common type, but his initials are carved in the handle. He was wearing it when he called at the castle last night, remember?"

"Yes. So he probably was helping the undertaker and somehow lost it. That's a relief. Did you find the grave?"

"Aye, it's all ready." She looked down at the knife, still frowning. "It doesn't make sense . . . Look, we'd better get back to the castle now, but when we've done all we can for Mrs. McAllister, I'd like to drop in on Dugald again. If we find him, he has a lot of explaining to do."

§   §   §

They didn't find him. That evening when they reached his house, they stopped the car at his door and knocked loudly. But there was no answer, so they went in and found the house just as they had left it, with nothing to indicate that Dugald had returned since their last visit.

They took advantage of the daylight still remaining to search his grounds as well, but they found nothing there and learned nothing at the village shop when they enquired. Frustrated and worried, they drove back to the castle.

"Maybe he'll show up at the funeral tomorrow," suggested David as they pulled into the car park.

"Aye, maybe. And if not, we can ask Mr. MacDonald if he has seen him. Anyway, I can't think of anything more we can do tonight. We'll just have to wait." Taking a deep breath, Sandy looked out over the countryside where long daylight continued to linger.

"It won't be dark for a wee while yet," she observed. "Let's walk up to the burn and see if we can figure out what Wally Morrison was up to this morning."

"Good idea. We might as well be doing something."

The ground was soft and boggy, but Sandy seemed to know just where to step for firm footing. David followed her, trying to step in her footprints. But he slipped off twice, so by the time they reached the burn his feet were squelching in his shoes. The stream chuckled and tumbled over a stony bed, then opened out into a peat-darkened pool.

Sandy looked back at the tower. "It must have been here, don't you think?"

He nodded. "I would say so. See anything?"

She shook her head. They patrolled the stream above and below the pool, but found nothing out of the ordinary. Then Sandy put her hand into the turbid water of the pool.

"Ouch," she squealed, "that's cold! Oh, well, here goes." She plunged her arm into the water.

"My feet are wet anyway," volunteered David. "Maybe if I go wading I'll step on something."

"You'll freeze," she warned, but he removed his shoes and socks and rolled up his jeans anyway. She was right, the water was frigid. He waded about for a few minutes, feeling around with his feet. Then he climbed back up the bank, shivering.

"If there's anything in there, it can stay

where it is," he decided. "Any luck over there?"

"No." Sandy pulled her arm out of the stream. "And if he was putting something in here, I'm sure he would leave it near the edge where he could retrieve it again without going wading."

"Now you tell me!" David dried his feet and legs as well as he could with his already damp socks, and thrust his feet back into his wet shoes. "Ugh! Maybe our friend Wally has a fetish about washing his face in peat water in the morning. Guaranteed to wash the cobwebs away."

"It would do that all right," Sandy laughed. "I'll bet it *was* something as innocent as that. I'm afraid our past adventures are making us paranoid."

"I have another idea." David was looking up to the nearby hilltop. "Now that we're here, let's take a look at the cairn up there, where Willie claims the fairies live."

Sandy hesitated. "It's getting late. It will soon be too dark to see much."

"There's not much to see anyway, is there? Just a pile of stones."

"More than that. It's a chambered cairn, I believe, so there's a room under the stones."

"Oh?" David was intrigued. "Too bad I haven't got my flashlight with me. Let's go take a quick look anyway."

Sandy agreed reluctantly. They ascended the

hill in the gathering gloom. The wind had come up and was whipping the heather about their ankles. It whistled through the bracken and moaned across the moor.

Suddenly they stopped short. Sandy clutched David's hand. "Do you hear that?"

He nodded dumbly. He heard it all right — the sound of unearthly music rising and falling on the wings of the wind.

"The wind in the stones," he whispered. "That's what you said."

She nodded. "That's what it is." But she didn't believe it, and neither did he.

For a moment they listened, enthralled. David felt the hair on the back of his neck rising. "Come on," he whispered. "Let's take a look."

Sandy hung back for a moment, then let him lead her closer. The flattened cone of stones was black against the darkening sky when they stopped.

The music was louder now, a haunting accompaniment to the song of the gale, like a thousand tunes played in harmony by some mystical being on a supernatural instrument.

"Let's come back later," shivered Sandy. Her voice was unsteady. "In the daylight. With a flashlight."

"I'll bring more than a flashlight," David promised as he turned and followed her quickly down the hill. "I'll bring a sprig of rowan in the form of a cross!"

11

The next morning Sandy and David were up early again. With no guests to be avoided, they made quick time once again descending into the dungeon and squeezing into the hollow wall. This time David ignored the ladder leading up into the tower. Instead he shone his light into the dark recesses beyond.

For a moment he could see nothing. Then he noticed what appeared to be a shadow on the inside wall. He edged past the ladder. In the narrowness of the gap he had to move sideways until he could kneel down to investigate. A moment later he rejoined Sandy in the dungeon.

"Guess what!" There was excitement in his voice.

"I've no idea. What?"

"The tunnel. Or *a* tunnel, at least. I couldn't see how far it goes, but there's a shaft leading off that way, under the tower."

"Well, well! Isn't that interesting." Her eyes gleamed. "Let me have a look." She took the light and went in to investigate. When she came back she was more thoughtful than thrilled.

"What do you think?" asked David. "Have we found out how the Laird escaped during the siege?"

"Probably," she acknowledged, "but that was hundreds of years ago. What's more important is that the tunnel has been used for something else fairly recently. There are some rather new timbers in there shoring up the roof. Did you notice that?"

"No, I didn't," he admitted. "Do you think maybe the smugglers used it to hide some of their goods?"

"It's possible. And maybe there's still something there that Ramshaw's come back for." She handed him the flashlight. "Let's check it out. I'll follow behind you."

The tunnel was small, just big enough to accommodate them on hands and knees, one behind the other. David crept into the black hole first. The light, probing the darkness ahead, told him only that there was nothing to see as far as it reached. His hand slipped on the timbered floor, and he shone the light downward.

"Hey!" he exclaimed in surprise. "This floor's been greased!" His voice came back to Sandy muffled, hollow.

"Greased? Are you sure? Then it's definitely

been used for something. Can you go on?"

"Oh, sure, it's not that bad. It's pretty well dried up. But it won't do our jeans any good."

He crept ahead. It was all right at first. Apprehension came slowly. After a few minutes he began to feel that the walls were closing in on him. They weren't, of course. He could still raise his head a bit before it touched the roof. He could still bend his elbows out a little before they touched the sides. A very little. The light shone ahead, so it wasn't as if he was in total darkness. It must be worse for Sandy, coming behind him with her hand on his heel. What little light she could see must be distorted, almost blocked by his body.

No, it was all right, he told himself. If only he could stand up for a minute. If only he could reach out on either side to stretch his arms. But he couldn't. The walls were closing in . . .

He closed his eyes and took a deep breath. When he opened them the walls were still there, close, stifling. The air was stale. It's like a grave, he thought. But he pushed that thought aside.

He was beginning to get a cramp in his hip. The need to stand up crept over him. But he couldn't stand up, and he tried to push that thought aside too. Instead he lay down flat for a moment, stretching out. It felt good to stretch, and the cramp eased. But the walls were still there on either side, pressing in, suffocating.

Sandy bumped into him from behind. "What

is it? Are you all right?"

"Just a cramp." He was glad to hear her voice. "I'll be okay in a minute."

But he wasn't okay. He got back onto his knees and was aware only of the stale air, the confines of the walls pressing in on him. He wanted desperately to stand, to fling his arms about, just to experience freedom. But he was trapped. Cold sweat broke out on his body. He shivered.

"Sandy" — it took a great effort to keep his voice calm — "let's go back." He would have to back out, bit by bit, feeling his way . . .

"Is it the cramp?" she asked anxiously.

"No." Suddenly he wanted to scream at her, to move her fast. He had to get out of there *now*! He bit his lip hard, realizing with a shudder that he was on the edge of panic. He took a long, deep breath. "Get hold of yourself!" he muttered angrily. The sound of his voice shocked him back into sanity.

"What did you say?"

"It doesn't matter." He spoke calmly, but he knew that panic was only a breath away, kept back by a conscious effort. "Sorry, but I have to go back quickly."

"Okay, come on." Her hand left his foot and they both backed up, awkwardly. There was no room to turn around, no room for anything. It was agonizingly slow work that seemed to take forever. If only he could see where they were going. If only he could shine a light, pick out the entrance to the tunnel, that would mean space to spread out. But it was impossible. He wanted to yell out, to demand why they were taking so long to get out of this tomb. It took all his concentration to keep calm.

When at last he was able to stand up in the dungeon, it was as if a great weight fell from his shoulders. He reached up high, swinging his arms in an ecstasy of freedom. His whole body was shaking.

"Davie! What's the matter?"

He didn't answer for a moment. When he did, his voice was hoarse. "Claustrophobia! That's what it was. I never knew it would affect me like that. I darn near panicked in there. I felt like I was in a grave, like I had to stand up but there was no way I could."

Suddenly her arms were around him and she was holding him close. "I'm sorry. I didn't know. It must have been terrible. Do you want to get up out of here?"

He looked around at the four walls that formed the tiny dungeon and he laughed. "Oh, no, this is like a stadium after that tunnel. It was so — so confining. I couldn't take it."

The flashlight had fallen to the floor. In the dim light from it and from the shaft overhead they looked at each other. She loosened her arms. "Then perhaps I shouldn't be confining you."

He laughed, then caught her arms and

wrapped them around him again. "This kind of confinement I could take forever." He bent his head and kissed her gently, briefly on the lips. "Thanks, Sandy, for being so understanding. I'm sorry I was such a coward."

"Coward! You're not that, David Mc-Crimmon. Don't you ever say that. I've seen you in some pretty tight corners before now and I know you're not a coward." She reached up and kissed him again, just an elfish touch of her lips, then stepped back from his arms. "Let's climb up to the top of the tower," she suggested. "We can sit up there and figure out what our next move will be."

Up in the clean air, with the big sky above him and the moors stretching to the horizon on all sides, David took a long, luxurious breath.

"If there's something hidden in that tunnel, I'm not going back in after it," he declared. "But I didn't see any sign of anything." He looked down ruefully at his stained jeans. "How do you suppose they used it?"

"I don't know. The grease suggests they slid something along the floor. Perhaps they stored things in boxes and shoved them into the shaft, then pulled them out again using a rope when they wanted to get at them. But the way into the tunnel is so narrow and awkward, I don't see how they could have used it much. Not for guns or that sort of thing at least, and we know they were smuggling arms to Ireland."

"So," said David, "if the tunnel really was being used, it seems likely there must have been another entrance."

"Yes, another entrance or exit. The tunnel originally afforded the Morrison laird an escape route, so where did he come out?"

"Let's see. The tunnel leads under the tower, going in that direction." They both leaned over the parapet and looked down. "It seems to be straight enough, so that would take it . . . "

David pointed down to the supposed location of the tunnel, then lifted his finger up, still pointing along what he judged to be a straight line. It pointed directly at the crest of the rise, straight at the cairn. Their eyes met.

"Of course!" said Sandy. "The fairy knoll. The *sithean*."

He nodded slowly. "You said there's a room of some sort under those stones, didn't you? So it could be. Perhaps it wasn't just fairies that lived there. But what about the music? We both heard that."

Sandy shook her head. "I don't know. And I suppose there's only one way to find out. What's the time?"

He glanced at his watch. "Breakfast time. We'll have to leave it till after the funeral now."

12

The Morrisons and Timothy Stevens attended the funeral and afterwards reclaimed their rooms. There was no sign of Dugald MacGregor, nor did the funeral director have any news of him.

"So how come his *sgian dhu* was lying in the grass in the cemetery?" wondered David. He and Sandy had left the castle after the service and were crossing the moor below the old wall, heading for the cairn.

Sandy shrugged. "The cemetery is open to the public and he has relatives buried there. I suppose it's possible that he went there to visit them."

"No. He wouldn't cut you off in the middle of a telephone conversation because of a sudden urge to visit the dearly departed, now would he? I don't like it at all. Something's happened to him."

"I'm afraid so too. Aulay probably recognized

Ramshaw and was killed for it. Dugald recognized him and has disappeared." She looked at David with eyes suddenly wide. "*We* have to be very careful, Davie."

"I know it. Especially after what we did to him before. If we get in his way again he's going to be as mad as a hornet. Sandy, I think we should go to the police with what we have before it's too late."

She hesitated, then nodded. "I think you're right. If we don't find anything up here at the cairn, I don't know what more we can do anyway. We may be on the wrong track altogether, for all we know."

David glanced once more over his shoulder, but no one was following them. They were beginning to climb the rise, stepping carefully over the peat hags. The burn babbled down the hill not far away, and the wind whipped at his clothing. The wind. Would they hear the music again? He stopped.

"I forgot the rowan to safeguard us from the fairies." He wasn't sure whether or not he was speaking in jest.

"Never mind, I brought some from the tree in the garden." Sandy grinned guiltily. She held up a small twig with several leaves on it. "Notice that it's not in the form of a cross though. I'm not really superstitious."

"Not much." He laughed and walked on. "Your prayers have gotten us out of tight spots before now. I think I'd rather rely on those."

The breeze freshened, and with it came the music. They were almost there when they heard it once more, an unearthly, haunting harmony wafted on the wind. They hesitated, looking at each other, puzzled and apprehensive. "Come on," said Sandy. "Let's solve this riddle once and for all."

Hand in hand they circled the cairn. On the far side was a low, wide gap. Flashlight ready, they crept inside.

For a moment they were aware only of the sound that swelled and drummed in their ears. David swung the light around, over the stones that formed the walls and roof. It was a dry-stone structure, with many gaps between the stones that had stood for centuries without mortar or buttress.

The light came to rest on the source of the music.

"For heaven's sake!" said Sandy in amazement. "A harp!"

A harp it was, standing there by itself; a harp, but with no visible harpist. Only the ghostly fingers of the wind, whistling through the gaps, plucked and sang through the strings, and the natural accoustics of the vaulted roof swelled the sound to orchestral fortissimo.

For a moment they stood and stared in stunned silence. Then Sandy stepped forward and turned the harp, just a little. Immediately the sound died to a melodious murmur.

"It's a Celtic harp," she said in awe. "What a beautiful instrument!"

"It sure is," agreed David. "But what in the world is it doing here?"

"It's scaring people away, that's what it's doing. See, it was placed to catch the prevailing wind in just the right way to make the most noise. The only people likely to wander this way are people like Willie Meenie Craig who have heard the old tales and still believe the old superstitions."

"I know what you mean," teased David. "People who carry sprigs of rowan for protection."

She didn't laugh, but nodded, looking at the twig in her hand. "You're right. But Willie put the rowan over her door. After hearing this sound she wouldn't dream of coming in here, even *with* rowan in her hand."

"So it worked — it kept people away. There must be something here worth protecting."

"Must have been at one time anyway. Remember, Willie said she hadn't been near here for years until the day she heard the music. This harp could very well have been placed here before Ramshaw was arrested. Probably what it's hiding is the entrance to the tunnel he was using in his smuggling operations."

They found the entrance a few minutes later. Stones and dirt which had apparently been disturbed on the floor led them to an iron plate. Below it was a shallow well from which the tunnel led off into the darkness. The well was empty.

They sat back on their heels and looked at each other.

"Another blank," sighed David. "Well, let's see. We know how the ghost got into the tower. We know how the Morrison laird escaped when his castle was under siege. We know how the fairy music was produced. But what good has it all done us?"

Sandy rubbed her forehead in perplexity, leaving a black smudge. "The only place we haven't looked is the entire length of the tunnel. And I don't believe there's anything there. The smugglers would have cleared it out before they left. No, this something we're searching for was hidden somewhere else by Ramshaw."

"But when he came back for it, it was gone. After he escaped from prison he never intended to stay here for long, I'm sure, yet he was here at least long enough to be recognized by both Aulay and Dugald. So he must have had to search for it just like we are."

"And as far as we know, he hasn't found it yet. So maybe we can still beat him to it. Where do we look now though?" Sandy stared thoughtfully at her feet. "Who do you think took this thing from its original hiding place?" she asked.

"Aulay," David answered without hesitation. "He had to have been the ghost."

She nodded her head. "Yes, I'm sure we're right about that. But why wouldn't he have turned his find over to the police?"

"Maybe Ramshaw caught up with him before he had a chance."

Sandy considered that. "So Aulay had the thing, but not for long, and he hid it in a new hiding place. Wouldn't the obvious suggestion be to search his room in the castle?"

"The police have already done that, haven't they?"

"Not really. They checked for papers — a will or whatever — but I doubt if they had any reason to give it a thorough search. And if Ramshaw is one of the guests, he won't have had much opportunity to get in there since the police finished. So if we act quickly we may get lucky."

"Let's go," David said, rising as he spoke.

They emerged from the cairn into daylight. Away to the south the hills were hidden behind a blanket of mist creeping across the moor. Above them the watery sun was losing a half-hearted battle with pregnant clouds.

A movement below caught David's eye. He pulled Sandy back.

"Look!" His voice was low. "There's Wally Morrison again. Back at the creek."

The American was in the act of rising from his knees beside the pool. He lifted a satchel, obviously empty, and slung it over his shoulder. They watched from the shelter of the cairn as he turned and walked back towards the castle.

"Now," said David in anticipation, "maybe we can learn something concrete about one of our suspects, at least."

Mist dampened their faces by the time they reached the spot where Wally had knelt by the brook. At first they could see nothing.

"Well, here goes again." Sandy rolled up her sleeve and knelt down by the water.

"Wait a minute. I can see something over there. Look." Something gleamed below the surface of the creek and kicked the tumbling water into a miniature cascade. David reached over and pulled it out.

For a moment the two of them stood and stared at it, there in his hand. Their eyes met and held for a moment, then merriment broke out in a gale of laughter.

"Beer!" gurgled Sandy. "That's what he was doing — cooling his beer in the burn! And to think we imagined him up to all kinds of nefarious deeds. I hope he doesn't find out what we thought. He'd have a fit."

"We'll have to be especially nice to him in the future to compensate for our suspicions," grinned David. He lowered the beer cans back into the water. "Typical American. Can't stand warm beer. Well, he's ingenious. That creek — pardon me, burn — will certainly keep it cool for him. Let's hope *all* our suspicions are as groundless as that one."

They turned their steps towards the castle again through the thickening mist. Fine rain was running down their faces, soaking their sweaters.

"I'm going to change," said Sandy. "Do you know where Aulay's room is? I'll meet you there in ten minutes with the keys."

Aulay's "room" was actually a suite that was to have been his permanent home. It had a small kitchenette, a bedroom that was not much larger, and a living room.

They started their search in the sparsely furnished living room. The only remarkable item in it was Aulay's bagpipes. They sat on the floor beside their case looking strangely forlorn, the drones, still intact, leaning against the wall.

"Look at that," whispered Sandy. "They look lost, don't they?"

David nodded. "I wonder what will become of them." He stood in silence a moment, then shook himself and said, "Well, we'd better not waste any time. Why don't you start with the chesterfield, and I'll tackle the desk."

There was nothing unusual in the desk, nothing behind the row of books on the shelf above it, nor in the books themselves.

Sandy had turned from the chesterfield and chairs and was on hands and knees feeling the carpet. She looked up. "No luck?"

He shook his head. "Nothing yet. There's just

the stereo and record rack to go in here. Then we'll try the kitchen."

The kitchen, used only for making tea and snacks, produced nothing. The bedroom took a little longer, but there too they drew a blank. They returned to the living room, disappointed.

"Well," said David, "it was a good idea, but now what? I think we'd better go to the police and tell them everything that's happened, then leave it up to them."

Sandy nodded reluctantly. "I suppose you're right. But I feel somehow as if we're letting Aulay down." She looked once more around the little room. Her eyes lit on the bagpipes. "At least I can put those away properly for him. It'll only take a minute."

She knelt beside the pipes, twisted the bass drone, lifted it and tilted it to lay beside the bag. Then she gave a startled, breathless cry.

"Oh, my goodness! Davie!"

"What is it?"

She was sitting back on her heels, staring open-mouthed at her hands. Dumbly she held them up for him to see.

"Wow!" he breathed in awe. "Where on earth —?"

"They were in the drone," she whispered, unbelieving. She stood up shakily. "Do you think — do you think they're *real*?"

He nodded. "They must be. That's what Ramshaw's come back for. Diamonds! Diamonds worth —"

"Worth a fortune. That's right!" The sudden voice came from behind them.

They spun around. Captain Reginald Moss was standing in the doorway, with an automatic pistol in his hand.

13

For an instant David stood frozen. Thoughts flashed through his mind in lightning succession: the realization that they held in their hands a prize of tremendous value; that the man with the gun must be the Laird of Ramshaw, the man who had already killed to get his hands on that prize and would not hesitate to kill again; that, incredibly, for a moment at least, the pistol was not pointing at either himself or Sandy but was, in fact, pointing at the floor. Now was his chance. The only chance he was ever likely to get.

He sprang forward, crashing into the Captain, hurling him backwards. The gun flew from the other's grasp.

"Sandy! Come on!" David caught his balance and swung around, grabbing Sandy's hand and pulling her out of the room. He slammed the door shut behind them.

"Just a minute, I have the key," gasped

Sandy, thrusting the diamonds at David. With shaking hands she pulled it from her pocket and slid it into the keyhole. It turned in the lock just as the handle rattled. A shouted curse sounded from within.

"Stop! Wait a moment!" The door shook with fierce pounding. "Let me out!" But they were already running down the hall, down the stairs.

"To the car!" panted David. "We've got to go to the police now."

They dashed past a startled Wally Morrison, almost knocking the pipe from between his teeth. Irene squealed in alarm. David and Sandy ignored them both and ran out the door, then sped across the car park to Sandy's Nova.

With a shriek of protest from the tires, Sandy backed out, narrowly missing a silver sports car parked behind them. She wrestled the car onto the road, then tramped on the accelerator. The road gleamed wet in the rain. She reached for the switch to activate the wipers.

"That silver sports car," said David. "Is that his?"

She nodded grimly. "I think so. It's a fast one by the look of it. And that door won't hold him for long." She swung the wheel hard as a sheep wandered on to the edge of the road. David grabbed the dashboard and held tight.

The Nova hurtled on. An approaching car pulled off to let them by, the startled driver acknowledging Sandy's quick wave of thanks.

Then they crested a low hill. A tractor was lumbering towards them. Sandy had no choice but to pull off into the nearest lay-by and wait while precious seconds slipped by.

"Come *on*," she urged, fingers tapping nervously on the wheel.

The driver of the tractor waved airily as he finally passed. The Nova jumped back on to the road behind him, and they were away again.

"Where do you think we're going?" asked Sandy suddenly.

David was puzzled. "You're driving. Don't you know?"

"Of course I know," she answered impatiently. "Just tell me where *you* think we're going."

"To Stornoway. Isn't that the nearest place to find the police?"

"Right. And Ramshaw/Moss will figure the same, so he'll be heading there as fast as he can. He has a good chance of catching us too. So we won't go there."

As she spoke she braked hard. The car slewed on the wet pavement, but she wrestled it around onto a side road. This one was even narrower, with bad pavement and infrequent lay-bys.

David looked back anxiously. A car went by on the other road, a maroon Volvo, but it was going towards the castle. "No sign of anyone coming after us."

Sandy nodded. "I hope I've done the right

thing. This will take us to the main Stornoway-Tarbert road. By the time Ramshaw figures out where we've gone, we should be almost in Tarbert."

They plunged down a grade that took them out of sight of the other road. That felt safer, but they were forced to slow down to avoid water-filled holes of indeterminate depth. Here and there the road led between stone dikes that squeezed in on them. In one of these narrow spots a flock of sheep brought them almost to a halt. Only a blaring horn and gentle nudging with the bumper persuaded the animals to break into a shambling run. When they finally disgorged and scattered to either side of the road, Sandy and David were sweating with impatience.

It seemed liked forever before they finally ground to a halt at the main road. A sign pointing to the left and right read *Steornabhagh* and *Tairbeart*.

"What on earth's that?" asked David.

"Gaelic, of course," answered Sandy. "Stornoway and Tarbert." She let a car go by, then swung into its tracks.

This was a two-lane road so they made good time, passing the few vehicles travelling in their direction with little trouble. And when the road abruptly narrowed to a single lane, the surface remained smooth and fast, the lay-bys frequent.

They were into the hills now, bare, rocky hills whose summits vanished in the mist. The road climbed steadily, then wound around the shoulder of a hill. The water of a loch gleamed far below. They plunged down, careening around a hair-pin bend.

Below them the road doubled back again so that they looked down on a lorry lumbering towards them. Sandy went on as far as she dared, then pulled into a lay-by. As the lorry inched by, growling up the grade, David looked back and tensed. Behind them a silver sports car was starting down the hill. It was travelling fast.

He was about to speak, but hesitated. Sandy was already driving about as fast as she dared. And besides, there were lots of silver sports cars. But when two approaching drivers, sensing the urgency in Sandy's driving, pulled off into lay-bys to let the Nova by, then stayed where they were because the other car was coming up so close behind, he knew he had to warn her.

"I think we're being chased." It was an effort to keep his voice calm.

"Oh, no!" She risked a quick glance in the mirror. "That car. How in the world . . .?" Her fingers tightened on the wheel and she hunched forward in her seat, urging the car to greater speed. The accelerator was already pressed to the floor.

They flew along the shore of Loch Seaforth, but then they were climbing again. The water of the loch dropped away almost vertically below them. The sharp incline took its toll, and the car slowed perceptibly. Sandy geared down, then braked hard for a sudden turn. The car swerved wildly. She had to drop to bottom gear, then gradually increased their speed through a long, straight climb. The water dropped further away, the hills beyond lost in the clouds.

Ahead of them another lorry inched its way up the mountain, blocking the single lane. David looked back. Their pursuer had made the last turn and was gaining.

"Sound the horn," urged David. "He'll pull off."

Sandy shook her head. "Would you, if you were driving that thing up a grade like this? We'll either have to wait or pass." She nosed the car over so she could see past the truck. Spray from the dual wheels blinded her for a moment, but the wipers fought against it.

The car behind was gaining fast. David could see that there were two people in it. One, he was sure, was Captain Moss. "We may have to take the chance," he warned.

A lay-by came into view ahead. As the lorry snarled along beside it, Sandy sounded a warning on her horn, pulled into it and tramped on the accelerator. Was the lay-by long enough to give them room and time to pass?

They were beside the rear wheels, lost momentarily in a swirling mist. When they emerged they realized for the first time that this was an articulated lorry, a long one. They drew alongside the drive wheels, then the cab. But the end of the lay-by loomed close. Beyond it, a sheer

116

cliff dropped to the loch far below.

For one fleeting instant Sandy hesitated, her foot poised to release the accelerator and stab the brake. Then with a desperate prayer, she committed herself and buried the accelerator in the floorboards. The front wheels of the lorry were beside her, the drop to the loch only metres away. At the last possible second she swung the car back in front of the truck, clearing the huge front end by centimetres.

The transport's horn blared angrily, but Sandy and David were past caring about that. An empty road lay ahead, and the lorry filled the road behind them, blocking the way for their pursuers.

The Nova gained speed, still climbing. They took another sharp curve, then saw the lorry far below them, the silver sports car snapping at its heels. They climbed until the mist hid everything below from view. The harsh hills surrounded them, closing in. They were alone in a clinging wet world.

The road was straight now, gleaming black. Their pounding hearts started to slow. But suddenly a stag stepped out of the haze, antlered head high. It stood proudly, directly in their path.

With a cry, Sandy stood on the brake. The car screeched and swerved. Safety belts snapped tight around shoulders and waists. The stag bounded away.

The car lurched from the road. A rock loomed

ahead, and Sandy was unable to twist the wheel far enough. One fender struck hard. The car came to a crunching stop.

The two passengers stepped out, shaken, wordless. One look at the car told them they were going no further that way. Sandy reached in and switched off the ignition. David looked up the road both ways. They were still alone.

"All right," said Sandy heavily, "I think it's time to head for the hills."

The hillside was a desolate graveyard climbing into the weeping clouds. Massive boulders hunched like headstones in a long-abandoned burial ground. Every wrinkle in the hard rock face ran with tears, and tendrils of mist lingered and writhed like ghosts of the long departed.

Sandy and David ran as fast as the slippery slope and fragmented rock permitted, away from the road, climbing up into the shelter of the massive boulders and mist that covered the hillside.

Below them the silver sports car soon came into view. It swerved to a stop beside the Nova and two men emerged. They were examining Sandy's car when yet another automobile, a maroon Volvo, pulled up beside them. Two men appeared and were welcomed by the erstwhile Captain Moss.

David and Sandy, crouched behind one of the boulders, exchanged glances.

"He must have called in his old gang," surmised David. "They'll be after us in a minute. There aren't many ways we could have gone."

If their pursuers had been in any doubt about where to look, those doubts were immediately dispelled. When David and Sandy turned to resume their flight, they dislodged loose stones that tumbled downhill, gathering others in their path to create a miniature landslide.

"That's torn it," muttered David. "They've seen us now."

They ran, climbing over grey conglomerate outcrops, feet sliding on the wet rock face. Every pucker in the hillside channelled another stream of water into a roaring burn. Slowly they worked their tortuous way up the foreboding face of the mountain.

Their pursuers were doubtless still following, but they were now lost below in the mist. David pulled Sandy into the shelter of a corrie cradled between high cliffs. She brushed dripping hair back from her forehead, breathing heavily.

"So far so good," she gasped breathlessly.

"Good isn't the word I had in mind," retorted David. "This is not my idea of a pleasant vacation."

"Oh, come on," protested Sandy with forced cheerfulness. "Look at it this way. You're hill walking in the Hebrides. People pay good money to do that."

"Sure they do. But they dress for the part, they have a compass, and if they have any sense they wait for good weather. And they don't have an angry Laird of Ramshaw coming after them with a gun. What's the next step?"

"We don't have much choice, do we? We keep going. But it's not so bad. Put yourself in Ramshaw's place. He's after two people he can't see who could be anywhere in these hills, hiding in any of these corries or behind any of these boulders, and its going to be dark before long. I wouldn't be surprised if he gives up soon."

"I would," countered David morosely. "He risked his life to come here for the diamonds I have in my pocket. He's not about to give up that easily. Besides *we're* the ones he's after, and that's an added incentive. He has an old score to settle with us. If I were him I'd at least leave a man or two to patrol the road, because if we have any sense we'll try to work our way back down there. There's no future in these hills, as far as I can see."

"We'll be all right," persisted Sandy. "We're here for the night anyway, whether we like it or not. Come on."

A little further on, a tongue of scree licked out from the mouth of a gully. They crossed the tumbled fragments of rock and followed them into a narrow, twisting ravine. The gorge was almost filled by a brawling burn that leapt and swirled and overran its natural channel. They struggled along beside it, feet squelching, clothing sodden. Here and there lurking stones reared up to trip them or moved beneath their feet, staggering them knee-deep into the rushing stream.

Miserable, hunched against the elements, they groped their way along, not knowing where they were going, their only objective to stay ahead of their pursuers.

David raised his head in yet another effort to see where the gorge was leading them. The mist lifted at that moment, just a little. David blinked rapidly, dashing the water from his face.

"Sandy," he demanded with new, half-strangled hope, "is it customary to see mirages in these parts?"

"What did you say?" She stopped so suddenly that he bumped into her. "Mirages? Aren't they a desert phenomenon?"

"Then I'm hallucinating. I just thought I saw a house a little further up the hill. What would a house be doing in this God-forsaken wilderness?"

"Where?" she cried eagerly.

"Up there. Can't see it now for the mist. Is it possible?"

"Oh, yes, it's possible. It could be a bothy."

"A what-y?"

"A bothy. A cottage that's been put there for deerstalkers or hill walkers who need shelter. I was hoping we might find one, but I didn't say anything in case we were disappointed. Can you lead the way to it?"

"Sure can!"

With new energy they left the stream behind

and began to climb the side of the ravine. At one point they came face to face with a sheer precipice that towered above them. They laboured along its base until the rock face gave out and they were able to scramble up a steep incline.

Suddenly the hillside levelled out into a plateau, and there was the bothy awaiting them. Solid stone walls promised warmth and shelter. Half fearfully, Sandy tried the door and sighed with relief when it opened to her touch. By mutual consent, before entering the haven, they stopped to look back.

Patchy mist clung to the mountain face and reached down into the ravine below. Here and there the rushing stream was barely visible. Far behind, the gap by which they had entered was hidden by the mist and the gathering gloom of night.

"I wonder where Ramshaw is." David spoke for both of them. "If they see the cottage they'll know we must be here."

"They might miss it," said Sandy hopefully. "We could easily have passed by below without seeing it ourselves."

"Yes, that was a stroke of luck. The mist lifted at just the right moment."

"It wasn't luck," declared Sandy positively. "It was an answer to prayer. Let's make the most of it."

14

It was almost dark inside the bothy. The fading light of day barely penetrated the three small windows.

"There should be a lamp here somewhere," Sandy said. "Ah, there it is. And matches." The soft flame of a coal-oil lamp flared, then settled into a subdued glow. It showed them several chairs, a table and, most importantly, an iron stove.

"Great," breathed David. "Is there anything to burn?"

Sandy lifted the stove lid. "It's all set to go at the touch of a match. That's the way you're supposed to leave these buildings, ready for the next climbers who need shelter. And there's more peat over in the corner to keep the fire going. There might even be some food around."

"There is," announced David as he explored a cupboard. "Some packets of oatcakes. And what's this? A tin of soup! And some tea bags."

"Well, there you are. What more could you ask?" Sandy struck a match and watched the eager flame lick at the kindling. "Put the kettle on, Davie."

"Not much point. It's empty."

"So fill it, chowder head."

David looked around. There was no water supply in the house. "I suppose I could wring out my sweater," he suggested.

She giggled. "We don't need that much. You'll have to go outside. There's plenty out there."

There was plenty, but the burn was far below and the mist-like rain too fine to catch. However, a few minutes' search revealed a waterfall that plunged down the hill and leaped happily into the kettle.

Before re-entering the cottage, David paused by the door and looked back. Far behind, near the opening that had led them into the ravine, he thought he saw a pinpoint of light. He waited, hoping he had been mistaken. No, there it was again. He watched for a moment. If it was moving at all, it was doing so very slowly.

"They're coming," he announced as he stepped inside, closing the door quickly behind him. "But they're still a long way off."

"Oh." Sandy had removed her sweater and hung it up. Drops of water fell from it and sizzled on the stove. "Do you think they've seen the cottage?"

"No way of knowing. With any luck we'll have time for soup and a cup of tea anyway. I'll keep watch while you rustle up some grub."

"Okay." She took the kettle from him. "But stand here by the stove for a few minutes and hang your sweater up. We might as well get as dry as we can while we have the chance. Does the lamplight show through the window?"

"Not yet, but it will when it gets really dark. We'll put it out as soon as we can."

They stood close together, soaking up the warmth. David was tempted to remove his shoes and socks, but the prospect of putting them on again while they were still damp did not appeal to him, so he left them on.

"Thank God for whoever invented bothies."

"I've already done that," Sandy told him. "Were you surprised when Captain Moss turned out to be Ramshaw, Davie?"

"Not really. I suppose he's the most likely of the three. Those eyes are just too green to be genuine. I think he must be a little peeved at us right now."

"Yes. And he's already killed Aulay for getting in his way. Maybe Dugald too." Sandy shivered.

"Dugald! I wonder . . . You know what a good way to get rid of a body is? I read it in a detective story once. You put the body into a grave that's already been dug and is waiting for a funeral. That way it's buried underneath a coffin, and the chances of it being discovered are — well, infinitesimal."

Sandy looked at him in growing horror. "His *sgian dhu* was found in the graveyard and Aulay's grave was already dug. Do you think . . .?"

"You checked the grave. What do you think?"

"I — I just glanced in to see that it was ready. I didn't look closely. Something *could* have been —" She didn't finish the sentence. "When we get back —" She didn't finish that either. They were a long way from getting back.

"We need a saucepan and a can opener for the soup," she decided practically. "Then you'd better keep watch. Let's not give him a chance to make it four murders."

The soup, full of vegetables and chunks of meat, was delicious even though they hadn't waited for the water to heat properly. By the time it was gone the kettle was boiling merrily, so they made some "proper" tea and drank it with dry oatcakes in a darkness unrelieved even by the glow of the lamp. They sat by the window staring out. Now and then David slipped through the door to look and listen outside, but each time he reported nothing.

"Think you could catch some sleep?" he asked Sandy when he returned for the fourth time. "It looks as if they've missed us."

"I don't think so," she answered. "I'm too keyed up. How about you?"

He shook his head. "Same here."

"All right, I'll try. If I do drop off, give me an hour or so. Then maybe by that time you'll be ready to take your turn." She looked around for a comfortable spot to lie down, but there was only the bare floor. In the end she sat where she was and leaned over the table, her head on her arms.

David reached over and tousled her hair. "Good luck, Sandy."

"I'll need it. Perhaps a good night kiss and a lullaby . . . "

"I don't know about the lullaby, but —" He stopped short. Then, "Oh-oh!" he breathed softly.

She looked up sharply. "What is it?"

"I think I saw a light. Just a flash. We'd better get ready to leave." He grabbed his sweater, handed hers to her, and checked his pocket. The diamonds were still there.

They stepped outside and listened. Nothing. Then they heard the sound of a dislodged stone tumbling down the hillside. It came from the direction in which they had approached the hut, not far away.

"Come on," whispered David. He caught Sandy's hand and led her away around the end of the building. They could make out the bulk of the hill before them, but not much more. David tried to recall the little about the terrain he had learned while looking for water for the kettle. "This way," he whispered.

The rain had ceased to fall, but the ground still ran with water. They stepped cautiously, but when the ground dropped away abruptly in front of them, David lost his footing.

"Are you all right?" Sandy asked anxiously, pulling him up.

"Yes. I don't remember that ditch being there. Come on."

They climbed for a long time, looking back over their shoulders every few minutes. Suddenly a light shone from beyond the cottage, silhouetting it.

It was possible to make out the shape of two men behind the light. They shouted, evidently hoping David and Sandy were still inside. Then when there was no response, they went in. The light shone through the tiny window.

David and Sandy stared at each other. "Well," said Sandy, "they know we've been there. And they can tell by the peat in the stove that we're not long gone. We'd better move on."

"Do you think if we ran back and asked them they'd lend us their light?" David asked in a forlorn voice.

She laughed, a small laugh. "Let's go."

It was the beginning of a nightmare, as they literally felt their way with hand and foot through the darkness. Danger waited on every side on the slippery, unknown mountain. At last they stopped in the shelter of a great boulder.

"Far enough," said Sandy firmly. "Unless we actually hear them coming, I vote we stay right here till daylight. We could walk over a cliff without even knowing it, like this."

"Okay. I'll bet Ramshaw and his pal are sipping tea and toasting their toes in front of the fire right now anyway. They're waiting for daylight to find us." David sighed enviously.

They sat together with their backs against the rock. David shivered, and so did Sandy. He put his arms around her and pulled her close.

"We *do* get into the darnedest situations," he muttered. "I think this God-forsaken wilderness is the worst yet."

"Not God-forsaken." Her voice was muffled against his coat. " 'If I make my bed in hell, even there shall thy right hand hold me.' That's from the Psalms. We'll be all right. Want to try for some sleep?"

"You're kidding! I'm sitting on a sharp rock, cold and wet, and you're talking about sleep. This is even worse than trying to sleep at a table. But you did mention a kiss and a lullaby."

"We'll have to forego the lullaby," she decided. "Ramshaw might hear us. But we could risk a kiss." She reached up and her lips were cool and brief on his. "Now snuggle up close and we'll wait for daylight."

They waited. Neither of them was able to sleep.

15

Daylight was a long time in coming. When it did at last, it gradually disclosed a desolate world of low, drifting mist that partially obscured mountain peaks, harsh, scree-covered slopes, tumbling waterfalls, and tortuous ravines. The dreary landscape did nothing to revive their spirits.

They stood up, sore and cramped, ate some oatcakes, and drank from a nearby burn.

"Now," said David, "which direction?"

Sandy shook her head, discouraged. "How would I know? The sun seemed to come up over there, but we can't even be sure of that. I suggest we just keep moving and see what happens."

"You mean we're lost?"

"Of course we are. But it's not as if we were in Canada. We're on an island, never far from the sea. If we keep moving, we're bound to come out of the hills sooner or later."

It proved to be later, much later. They

entered ravines that started downward promisingly, only to climb again or end abruptly against towering cliffs. They climbed a rock face, then followed the course of a foaming burn that brought them back, eventually, to their point of departure. But always they set out again doggedly, holding hands when the terrain permitted, grimly silent.

They were hungry and desperately tired when their luck turned. The sun came out, shining translucent on a shimmering world. A rainbow formed a perfect arc before them. They stood together in subdued awe as the landscape was transformed into a thing of beauty all around them.

Suddenly Sandy caught David's hand and pointed between two hills. "Look at that!" she whispered happily. "The sea!"

With rising spirits they pushed their weary bodies to renewed effort. The beckoning sea was still beyond many a slippery slope and agonizing climb. The position of the sun indicated that it was afternoon by the time they finally stood on the edge of a peat bog, the other extremity of which was washed by the whispering waves. In front of them ran a road.

"At last!" breathed David. "Thank God. The road."

"Not *the* road," corrected Sandy, frowning. "I mean, it's not the Stornoway-Tarbert highway we left yesterday. See, it's not in good condition at all. Do you know where we are?"

David shook his head. "Not a clue," he admitted.

"We've come right through the hills to the southwest coast. That's the Atlantic Ocean out there."

"How can you tell? All water looks the same to me."

"I know that the only road in existence in this area besides the highway is one that runs west from Tarbert along West Loch Tarbert, which is part of the Atlantic. The only thing is, I don't know where we are on that road. Tarbert might still be miles away."

"But at least we can hitchhike, or — Wait a minute. Isn't that the roof of a house just beyond that hill?"

"Oh, yes, it is! Let's go, Davie. If there's anyone there they'll help us."

It was a stone farmhouse set among several outbuildings, with chickens clucking in the yard and sheep roaming everywhere. A sign on a post informed passers-by that bed-and-breakfast was available within.

"Sandy," said David, "do you have any money on you?"

"Yes, a little. Are you thinking what I'm thinking?'

"Absolutely. I'm exhausted and famished. Would it make much difference if we took a few hours off to rest and eat?"

"It would make a lot of difference to us.

Ramshaw can go peddle his peaches for all I care right now."

At their approach, a man came out of one of the outbuildings. He eyed them curiously, obviously taking in their bedraggled appearance. "Can I help you?" he asked courteously.

"Yes, please," said Sandy. "We've been lost in the hills since yesterday, and we're rather tired and hungry."

"Aye, ye've come to the right place." He was too polite to question them further. "Come in, come in." He held the door open for them, ushering them into a small parlour where a peat fire glowed in a grate and easy chairs beckoned.

"Mairi will bring tea and a bite to eat in a few minutes," he promised. Moments later a round, cheerful woman bustled in.

"What's this Hector was telling me? Ye've been lost in the hills? Och, look at the two of you, soaked to the skin and aye worn out. Never mind, we'll look after you. I'm sorry we haven't the telephone and the car's broken down. Will there be anyone worrying about ye?"

They looked at each other. Ramshaw would undoubtedly be worrying about them, but probably no one else. The castle wasn't re-opening for tours until tomorrow.

"No," said Sandy, "we won't be missed. We'd be very grateful for a chance to sleep for a few hours at least."

"A few hours! A good night's rest is what ye

both need, after a meal and a hot bath. But the first thing ye must do is get out of those wet clothes. What are your names?"

"I'm Sandy. He's David."

"And I'm Mairi. You come with me, Sandy. We'll get you something dry to wear. Hector will look after David."

A few minutes later they were seated in a cosy dining room, with steaming cups of tea and plates of bacon, eggs, sausage and potatoes in front of them. Sandy was almost lost in an oversize bathrobe. David wore a shirt and pants just a little too big for him.

"I'm beginning to feel almost human again," sighed Sandy.

"Mmm. Me too." After that they were too busy for conversation.

"I think Mairi's right," observed David at last. "We should stay the night and forget everything until tomor—"

He stopped short at the sudden sound of voices in the hallway. They heard their names mentioned, but before they could react, the door opened and Hector looked in.

"Aye, they're in here," he said over his shoulder. Then, to David, "Here be some friends looking for ye."

Some friends! It could only be Ramshaw! David sprang up, looking wildly for some means of escape. But in their newfound comfort they had let their guard down. They were trapped.

A moment later they were gaping in amazement and relief, for it was not Captain Moss who pushed his way in, but Wally and Irene Morrison.

"Mr. and Mrs. Morrison!" David cried. "What are you doing here?"

"Looking for you." Irene caught his hand in a tight squeeze. "We're so happy to find you. We were sure you were in some kind of trouble." She enveloped Sandy in an awkward hug.

"But I don't understand," said Sandy when she had escaped from the hug. "What made you think —"

At that moment Mairi bustled in, and conversation became impossible until the Morrisons managed to assure her that they could not possibly stay for a meal. They were finally persuaded to sit down across the table from Sandy and David and take a cup of tea.

"You almost knocked both of us over when you came running down the stairs at the castle," Irene belatedly answered Sandy's question. "And then that awful Captain Moss came running after you with a *gun* in his hand! I couldn't believe it. He asked where you'd gone, but we were too surprised to tell him. We knew you'd taken off in the car though, so when we saw him do the same we decided to follow in case we could help."

Wally was filling his pipe. "Before long Moss was met by another car," he took up the story. "A Volvo. They stopped him and told him which way you'd gone, I guess. He went after you, driving fast. Too fast for us. We're still not used to driving on the wrong side of the road. Of course, it doesn't matter much on these single lane roads, but you do have to stop and think what to do when you meet someone at one of those lay-bys. Anyway, we lost him, then finally came across his car again stopped beside yours."

"At first we were afraid that he'd caught up to you," Irene broke in again. "But then we saw men walking along the road and two more climbing the hill, so we figured you'd got away. We didn't know what to do. We thought of going to the police, but what could we tell them? So we drove up and down that road for the rest of the day in case you came out of the hills, and then we tried again this morning.

"We were really getting worried. You still hadn't shown up, and Captain Moss hadn't come back for his car either. So finally we looked at the map and decided you just might make it as far as this road. We've been along here twice now. This time we decided to stop and ask these people if they had seen you. And here you are!" she finished triumphantly.

"Now," said Wally, pausing with a lighted match poised over the bowl of his pipe, "are you free to tell us what this is all about?"

"I guess we owe you that much," said David. "We're very grateful for what you've done to help us."

Between the two of them they told their story, while Irene's eyes grew wider and wider over her teacup. By the end of it she was gazing at them in disbelief. "Do you mean to say," she demanded, "that you have a fortune in diamonds just loose in your pocket?"

"That's right," nodded David. He reached into his pocket and spilled them out onto the table.

"Oh, look!" She spoke in an awed whisper. "Wally, aren't they — breathtaking!"

"Beautiful," Wally agreed calmly. "But the point is, what are you going to do now? Do you want us to drive you into Tarbert so you can tell all this to the police?"

"They canna go anywhere right now!" Mairi had come in and caught the last of Wally's words. "I do not know your business with the police, but these ones are dead on their feet. And their clothes will no' be dry for an hour or more."

"She's right," said Sandy. "We can't go anywhere just yet. But if you wouldn't mind . . ."

"Anything," offered Irene, eagerly. "We'll do anything to help."

"Then could you go to Tarbert and tell the police what we've told you, and ask them to come for us later? Give us four hours sleep anyway, if they won't wait till morning."

"Yes," said David, "and take these things with you." He scooped up the diamonds and held them out to Wally. "I'll be only too glad to get rid of them, and if the police have any doubts about your story this should convince them."

Irene and Wally exchanged glances. "I don't know," Wally murmured reluctantly, but Irene interrupted him.

"I think we should, Wally. They've been through such a lot, these two, and if it will help them . . . "

Wally gave in. "All right, if that's what you want, we'll do it. And we'll suggest to the police that they let you rest till morning. You do both look as if you need it."

The Morrisons left with the diamonds, and David and Sandy sat down to contemplate a well-earned rest.

"Whew!" sighed Sandy. "That's a relief."

And so it should have been — a relief. Yet David still had an uneasy feeling in the pit of his stomach, as if something were not right.

He looked at Sandy. She was nibbling on shortbread between gulps of tea, yet she too wore a worried frown.

"What's bugging you?" he asked.

"Well," she said slowly, "if the Morrisons could find us here, so can Captain Moss or Ramshaw or whoever he is."

David was startled. For a moment he examined his own thoughts. Was that what had been bothering his subconscious? No, he decided, there was still something else.

"I hadn't thought of that," he admitted. "You're right, of course. The diamonds are safe from him now, but we're not. And as far as he knows we still have them. Do you think we should persuade Mairi and Hector to lie for us and tell anyone who comes along that we were never here?"

"Yes, but we'll have to tell them everything. Agreed?"

"Sure, why not? We may need all the allies we can get."

So they related the whole story once again, and gave their host and hostess a description of Captain Moss. But Mairi and Hector decided to let no one in except the police themselves.

"What if someone comes along who wants bed and breakfast?" asked Sandy.

"Och, that'll be no trouble," Mairi assured her. "We'll tell them our rooms have been reserved for a family who will arrive later this evening. Now, Sandy, let us get you into yon warm bath, and when you're done David will be wanting his turn."

"If I'm still awake," David agreed. "But if I've fallen asleep don't bother to waken me."

So David went to wait in the little attic room he had been assigned. For a few minutes he looked out the window to where the road lay between the sea and the hills. It was empty.

Where's Ramshaw? he wondered. As Sandy had pointed out, if the Morrisons could find them, so would Ramshaw, sooner or later. But with the kindly Hector and Mairi standing guard over them they should be safe for the night, and the Morrisons were now well on their way to the police.

The Morrisons. Why had they taken such an interest in his and Sandy's affair? Their explanation seemed reasonable enough, and yet . . .

He thought about the two of them, typical American tourists. Irene, with her eager inquisitiveness and prattling tongue, so interested in everything; Wally, with a bit of a pot and a balding head, calmly filling his pipe.

Filling his pipe! Suddenly David paled. He stood transfixed, staring unseeing out the window. The pipe! He raised a shaking hand to his brow. Of course, the pipe! And that blunt thumb. And something else too. Something Wally Morrison had said. He remembered it clearly now. He *knew*.

"Oh, my heavens," he groaned. "We've done it this time!"

He turned and dashed out the door, ran down the stairs to the door of the bathroom and knocked urgently. "Sandy!"

"Yes, what is it?"

"I've got to talk to you. Now!"

"Just a minute." After only a brief pause she opened the door, still wrapped in Mairi's robe. The scented bath waited invitingly behind her. "Davie, what's the matter?"

"Sandy, we've goofed! We've played right into his hands. I don't know who Captain Moss is, but he can't be Ramshaw. *Because Wally Morrison is Ramshaw!*"

140

16

"What? What are you talking about?" Sandy stared incredulously at David. "That's impossible!"

"No, it isn't. Look." He paused. "We can't talk here. Let's go into your room for a minute."

She followed him and stood just inside her door. For a moment he stared out the window without saying anything. Then he turned to meet her disbelieving stare.

"Did you notice how Wally Morrison fills his pipe?"

"Fills his pipe! What on earth —? No, I didn't notice how he fills his pipe. How does he do it?"

"By pushing the tobacco into the bowl with his thumb, like this."

"Does he? I never noticed. And that makes him the Laird of Ramshaw? Davie, what are you talking about?"

He ignored her sarcasm. "The first time I saw Ramshaw he was sitting on a deck chair beside me on the *Skerryvore*. I would have had to turn to look at his face, but I had no trouble seeing his hands. They were in front of him, and he was using his thumb to fill his pipe. He had big, square hands and a — a blunt thumb.

"I've noticed Wally filling his pipe twice now, including tonight. It reminded me of something, but I couldn't place it. Until just now, when I suddenly remembered where I'd seen those hands before."

"But you can't say *those* hands," objected Sandy. "There must be lots of men with hands like that, and I'm sure some of them use their thumbs to fill their pipes. If that's all . . . "

"No, it isn't all. There's something else that I almost missed when it happened, but it stuck in my memory, just below the surface. Remember when I first met the — the guests, in the drawing room? All four of them were waiting for Mrs. McAllister to bring in the tea. They knew you because you had been their guide, but they'd never met me. So you introduced me. And do you remember what Wally said?"

She shook her head dumbly.

"He said, 'You must like it in Lewis to have come back again.' Now, how did he know I'd ever been here before? There's no way Wally Morrison of Toledo, Ohio would know that. But the Laird of Ramshaw knew it very well."

Sandy shook her head stubbornly. "Couldn't he have assumed you had been here before? If I remember correctly, I told him you would be working here for the summer, so he might have guessed that you had been —"

"No. Even if he thought that, which is nonsense, why would he say it? No, Sandy, Wally Morrison is Ramshaw. I'm absolutely certain now. Take away the padding, let his hair grow, add that moustache. Oh, yes, he's Ramshaw. And he's away with the diamonds, just like he planned."

Sandy was shaken. "Well, maybe, but then who is Captain Moss?"

David sat heavily on the edge of the bed. "Yeah, that's a good question. Who is he? I have a horrible feeling he's been a friend all along."

"Huh! Some way for a friend to act!"

"Wait a minute. Remember when he came into Aulay's room behind us? He had a gun, but it wasn't pointed at either of us. It was pointing at the floor, otherwise I wouldn't have jumped him the way I did. We just didn't give him a chance to explain, then or at any time since, did we?"

"No, we didn't." She passed her hand through her tousled hair in perplexity. "So what do we do now?"

David sighed. "We don't get any sleep yet, that's for sure. The Morrisons certainly won't be going to the police, so somehow we have to get to them. Even if we have to walk all the way. How far is Tarbert from here?"

"Twelve miles, Hector told me. We'd better

leave right away. Oh, well, I was of two minds about this bath anyway. I was afraid I might fall asleep in the tub."

"At least we've had a good meal and our clothes are a bit drier," David pointed out. "I'll go and ask Mairi for them now, and try to explain to her why we have to go."

When Sandy and David set out minutes later, it was over strong objections from their hosts. Hector had offered to go for them, but they'd turned him down with thanks.

"We couldn't rest anyway," explained David. "Knowing what we do, there's no way we could fall asleep. We have to be doing something, even if it *is* walking all the way to Tarbert."

"Och, ye willna have to do that. The Nicolsons have the telephone, just four miles down the road. You can call from there."

"Just four miles!" David's exclamation broke the silence long after they had left the farmhouse behind. "That's about seven kilometres!" he groaned.

"Look at it this way," said Sandy with forced cheerfulness. "We're walking on a flat road through level countryside this time — well, comparatively level anyway. And the wind is at our backs, not only helping us along, but reminding us that our clothes are still damp, thus keeping us awake. What more could you ask?"

"A ride would be nice," said David.

"Well, that's a possibility. This *is* a road, and

cars do come along here occasionally, I'm sure. Look, there's something now. Going the wrong way, of course, but at least it proves that there is mobile life in these parts."

The grey-bearded tractor driver waved at them as he passed, and the growl of his machine reached their ears long afterwards. But they were completely alone except for the ever-present sheep.

"It's just as well we didn't take up Wally's offer to drive us to the police," observed David. "We never would have gotten there. I wonder what he would have done with us?"

Sandy shivered. "I don't know. I wonder if Irene would have let him have his revenge on us, or would she have persuaded him to let us go and be satisfied with the diamonds."

"He couldn't afford to let us go. We know too much."

"Yes, I suppose so. I wonder who she is anyway. Ramshaw never had a wife."

"One of his old gang, I expect. They certainly played their parts well. That business of the beer in the burn, for instance. That was convincing. But even Ramshaw made one slip-up."

"If he hadn't —" She stopped abruptly and caught David's arm. He had seen it too. A car was approaching in the distance, a silver sports car. Then another appeared in its wake, a maroon Volvo.

"Well," said Sandy, "this is it. What do we do?

Head for the hills again, or wait here?"

David hesitated for only an instant. "We wait, and hope we're doing the right thing. I'm too tired to run any more."

They stopped where they were and waited beside the road, resigned to their fate.

The leading car slowed as it approached, as if it were suspicious. When it stopped, Captain Moss unwound himself from the driver's seat. For a moment he leaned on the open door, regarding them. Then he deliberately closed it, raised his hands in the air, and walked towards them.

"Well," he said, "why aren't you running this time?"

"I think," said David uncomfortably, "that we've made a mistake or two."

"Yes, I think you have. Where are the diamonds?"

"I hate to say it, but Ramshaw has them."

"You mean Ramshaw, as in Wally Morrison?"

"You know about him?"

"I do now. My men saw him patrolling the highway when you were in the hills, so I guessed. Should have known long ago, but he had me fooled."

"Who *are* you anyway?" broke in Sandy.

"Oh, sorry, I'm Captain Reginald Moss, R.N., but not retired. I'm in the Intelligence branch. Any ideas where our friend is now?"

"He headed for Tarbert about half an hour ago. That's all we know."

"Well, we certainly didn't meet him. All right, you ride in the Volvo with me and you can tell me all about it. We'll head back that way again."

When Sandy and David had finished their story, it was Captain Moss's turn to tell his. On Ramshaw's escape from prison, he had been sent to the castle to keep watch in case the prisoner returned there. The ghost stories, then Aulay's death convinced him that Ramshaw had indeed returned, and he had called for backup in case he was forced into a confrontation. He had reached more or less the same conclusion that Sandy and David had, that Ramshaw was looking for something to finance his future, and that Aulay's room would bear searching. After the funeral he had gone there to do so, but on approaching the room he had heard someone moving about inside. Believing it might be Ramshaw, he had unholstered his gun.

"But of course, it turned out to be you two. And I saw that you had found those diamonds, obviously the thing Ramshaw had come back for, and obviously very valuable. I should have pocketed the gun, but really, you know, you didn't give me a chance. First thing I knew I was flat on my back and you were gone. Damn fine work, young fellow."

David grinned sheepishly. "Sorry about that. We thought you must be Ramshaw."

"Don't apologize. And I can't blame you for giving the diamonds to Wally either. *I* never caught on that he was Ramshaw until my men told me how he had been watching the road while we were chasing you. And he thought of checking this road before we did, worse luck. Well, now we just have to catch the blighter!"

A few minutes later he touched the driver on the shoulder. "Stop at that house, driver," he ordered. "Now you two," he turned to Sandy and David, "this is a bed-and-breakfast establishment, and here's some money. You both need a good night's rest after your adventure."

"You mean that's it? We're out of it?" They looked at him in dismay. "But can't we do anything to help you?"

"Sorry, no. You've done enough already. It's out of your hands now. Leave it to the professionals. Sandy, give me your keys. I'll have your car taken care of, and it'll be at this door tomorrow morning so you can drive home. Now off you go. Forget all about this business, and have a good sleep."

Reluctantly they got out of the car and watched from the roadside as it drove off.

"Well," said David glumly, "talk about anticlimax! All that, and now we're supposed to just forget about it."

"Sent to bed like naughty children," Sandy sighed. "Well, I suppose that's what we are, in a way. If we hadn't butted in, Captain Moss would have solved the whole thing by himself."

"Not necessarily," said David. "He might or

might not have found the diamonds. Would he have looked in the bagpipe drones? And if he had, he would have taken them downstairs, and who was waiting down there? Wally and Irene Morrison. Captain Moss didn't know Wally was Ramshaw."

"Well, we're out of it now anyway. We'll just have to try and forget about it. But there is one good side. This bed-and-breakfast is run by old friends of Uncle Rory, Megan and Donald Mac-Innes, so I can vouch for the softness of the beds in there. And Ramshaw will never find us with them around to watch over us."

"That's great," nodded David. "But I don't know if I'm ready to get into one of those soft beds right now. I'm too keyed up."

"Me too," agreed Sandy. "I'm tired, but I don't think I could go to sleep yet. So let's go and make arrangements for rooms with Megan, then sit down on the shore for a while. It won't be dark for a bit."

§   §   §

"Could that be Donald coming now?" asked David. "Megan said she was expecting him home for dinner soon."

He and Sandy were relaxing on the shore of the bay. The road wound around the shore, and beyond it hills formed a clasp in which the water of the bay lay like a jewel. Two or three houses dotted the shoreline, and at the inner end of the bay one motor launch was moored. At the other end a narrow gap opened out to the Atlantic.

As he spoke David lifted his arm lazily to indicate a fishing boat just coming through the gap. She had a high prow, crossed booms amidships, and a lofty wheelhouse at the stern.

"Aye," answered Sandy, "that will be Donald and the *Silver Star*. He'll anchor her here while he and the crew eat, then take the day's catch on to Tarbert later."

They watched the little craft approach, her motion steadying once she was well inside the shelter of the bay. She came in quite close before the engine reversed and pulled her to a stop. Then a figure emerged from the hatch and advanced towards the bow.

David drew in his breath sharply. "What in blazes is *that*?" he demanded.

The figure was draped in oilskins with a matching hat, but it was the face that shocked the exclamation out of David — the grotesque, grinning gargoyle of a face.

"That is a man," said Sandy mildly. "He's wearing a mask to protect his face from the scalders."

"Scalders? What's that, another of your weird superstitions?"

She laughed. "No, scalders are real enough. They're jellyfish, and they sting like billy-o. They come in on the creels. If their stingers splash up into your face you feel like it's on fire, and they can blind you if you don't act fast. The men have found that Hallowe'en masks are the perfect protection."

Sure enough, the man on the deck pulled a mask off his head before he lowered the anchor. Then he and two other men came in to shore in a rubber dinghy. They pulled the little craft onto the beach, and two of them strode away towards one of the other houses nearby. The third man caught sight of Sandy and David and stopped.

"Well, Sandy MacLeod! What are you doing here?" He was a big man in a heavy roll-neck sweater and turned-down sea boots. He regarded them from piercing blue eyes. "Is your uncle in these parts?"

"No, we're just on a walking tour and have decided to stay here overnight. This is David McCrimmon from Canada. He's going to be working with me at Ramshaw Castle for the summer."

"Is he now? Welcome to the Hebrides, young fellow." David's hand was bruised by the other man's grip.

"Thank you. Did you have a good day's fishing?"

"Aye, a good day for the lobsters, but a bad day for the scalders. We're not finished cleaning them up yet, but they can wait and Megan can't. Would you like to take a look at our catch?"

David looked out to where the boat waited at anchor. "That would be great," he nodded.

"Fine. You take the dinghy out and have a tour of the *Silver Star*. Sandy can answer your questions, am I no' right, lassie? And I'll away and have my dinner."

While Donald strode away in a rolling gait, Sandy and David rowed the short distance to the *Silver Star*. Boxes of freshly caught lobsters, already nailed shut, were stacked on the deck and in the hold. Here and there beautiful, translucent jellyfish pulsated on the deck, and crabs scuttled guiltily between the crates.

"Steer clear of the jellyfish," warned Sandy. "Maybe we could help clean them up, but I'll show you the crew's quarters first."

There were bunks for six in the cramped cabin, three on either side of a folding table, in tiers, but how six men could move about in such a cramped space was beyond David's imagination. It was obvious, however, that only three of the bunks were in use for their original purpose. The other three were piled with oilskins and other personal effects. A little galley stove was at the end of the room, and the sink beside it held unwashed tea mugs.

"Of course," Sandy explained, "no matter how big the crew, they're not all in here at once. At sea someone has to be on the wheel, even while they're not actually busy with the lobsters. And in port they go ashore. Come on up to the wheelhouse."

There was barely room for the two of them to stand behind the wheel. A ship-to-ship/ship-to-shore radio was the only other thing in the cramped space, except for a pair of binoculars hanging from a nail. David took them down and focussed them out the window.

"Hey, these are great, really powerful! Let's go out on deck and have a look around."

There were several creels awaiting repairs in the close space behind the wheelhouse. David sat on one of these and swept the glasses slowly over the surrounding countryside, taking a closer look at the hills that encompassed the bay and the houses that dotted the shoreline. He inspected the sleek motor launch he had noticed earlier too. Two figures were busy at something on the deck. The glasses moved on, then wavered, came back, focussed again on the launch.

"No," breathed David, "it can't be. But it is!"

17

David lifted the binoculars carefully from around his neck and handed them to Sandy. He spoke slowly, trying hard to keep the excitement out of his voice.

"Look out at that boat," he instructed, "and tell me what you see."

"Why?" she inquired. "Is it something special?"

"Just look," he grunted.

She took a moment to adjust the focus, then lifted the glasses to her eyes.

"I see a smashing launch that must have cost a packet, with two men on her deck —"

She stopped short. David sensed the sudden tautness in her body. For a moment she was silent, then she said softly, her voice tight, "— one of whom is Wally Morrison."

"That's what I thought, but I couldn't believe it." David sighed, releasing his tightly held breath. He and Sandy looked at each other in amazement.

"So what do we do now?"

"Get hold of Captain Moss fast. But how? Could we use the radio in the wheelhouse?"

Sandy shook her head. "No, Ramshaw might be listening in. But Donald and Megan have the telephone. Davie, you keep an eye on that launch. I'll go ashore."

Sandy rowed quickly ashore and ran up to the house, while David turned his attention back to the launch. The two men had gone below, but any doubts David may have had were quickly dispelled as Irene Morrison came up on deck wearing the same wide-brimmed hat he had hidden behind the day he arrived at the castle.

Irene emptied something over the side of the launch and dallied by the rail for a few minutes, then disappeared below again. There was no further sign of life, and the deck was still empty when David heard the dinghy returning from shore. Sandy came aboard a moment later, followed by Donald.

"I couldn't reach Captain Moss," she reported, "but I got hold of the police and they know all about what's going on. They'll contact the Captain as soon as they can. In the meantime, guess what we're supposed to do."

"Go and have a good night's rest?" David's voice was glum.

"No, not this time. If that launch shows any signs of leaving, our job is to delay them as long as we can."

"*Delay* them! How in the world are we supposed to do that?"

"I have no idea."

"Och, I have a plan." Donald MacInnes had taken the glasses from David and turned them on to the launch. "And none too soon, I think. It looks as if your friends are preparing to leave. David, when I give the word, you switch on the motor in the bow and bring up the anchor."

He disappeared into the wheelhouse, and a moment later the engine clanked, sputtered and coughed into life. "Now," he called.

David flicked a switch and the anchor came up, dripping seaweed. Then the *Silver Star* cut through the water as Donald opened up the engine.

"Take over here, Sandy," Donald called from the window of the wheelhouse. "Steer for the gap. I want to see what that launch is doing. And David, you come and tell me what is going on here. Sandy's bits and pieces of the tale have not satisfied my curiosity at all."

Donald continued to study the other boat through the glasses while David recounted the story as briefly as he could. By the end of it Donald was shaking his head gravely.

"Aye," was his only comment, "this Ramshaw must surely be stopped from slipping out to sea, or he will away and begin anew. And you two will not be safe while he continues free."

"But how can we stop him?" asked Sandy.

"Block the gap," Donald answered briefly.

"Block the gap! But how? They won't just sit by and let us anchor in the middle of the channel."

"No, they won't," agreed Donald. "But if I'm stuck on a reef there won't be much they can do about it, will there?"

"Are you serious?"

"Aye, I am. We're close to ebb tide, so yon gap is very narrow indeed. A little deviation off course will put us nicely onto the rocks, and there we'll sit until the tide washes us off in about six hours. There'll be no room for Ramshaw and his launch to get by."

"But won't you damage the hull?"

"Och, no, not if I'm careful. A wee bit paint, that's all. The only damage," he added ruefully, "will be to my reputation as a seaman."

"That's right," said Sandy anxiously. "Anyone will know that you couldn't possibly make so bad a blunder."

"These people are strangers who don't know me. They won't be hard to convince. They've weighed anchor already. I'll take the wheel now, Sandy."

As they neared the gap, rows of gulls watched them for a moment, then took off with raucous maledictions. They moved into the channel carefully. On one side the hill rose steeply out of the sea, but on the other side the rock face shelved under the surface, sloping gradually, the receding tide revealing more and more rock and narrowing the navigable canyon.

For a moment they headed towards the deepest part of the channel, then Donald deliberately spun the wheel and eased back on the throttle. They waited, tense. There was a bump. The boat jolted back. A little more throttle brought the sound of protesting timbers from the hull. The boat stopped.

"That's it," said Sandy. "We're aground."

"Aye," agreed Donald, "but only just. He may offer to pull us off if he's in a hurry. Just a little more . . ."

The engine snarled again. The propeller bit into the water, thrusting ahead. The hull groaned, then shrieked in complaint. David held his breath, expecting to hear an inrush of water.

"That'll do it," said Donald cheerfully, cutting the engine. "We're here till the tide gets us off now, and nothing can get by. Where's that launch?"

She was coming towards them, suspecting nothing, at nowhere near the speed of which she was obviously capable.

"I think," said Donald in anticipation, "that we'll soon be hearing some pretty tall language."

That's right, thought David. In a few minutes the launch would reach them and — Suddenly he realized the peril he and Sandy were in. He spun round to her.

"Sandy, we can't just stand here and wait. We can't let Ramshaw see us!"

"That's right. We'll have to go below. Donald,

can you bluff them on your own?"

"Aye, away you go. Leave them to me."

Sandy and David descended the steep stair into the tiny cabin and pulled the hatch over their heads. Sandy found a light switch. They looked at each other.

David shook his head ruefully. "As I said before, we do get ourselves into the darnedest situations. Whoever would have thought of this? So what do we do now? Sit and wait?"

"We make tea," said Sandy. "When in doubt, make tea." She turned on the stove under the kettle as she spoke. "Otherwise there's not much we can do. I think Ramshaw's going to be plenty mad."

"No doubt about that," agreed David grimly. "I hope Captain Moss or the police or someone gets here fast."

They heard the approaching launch moments later, the low grumble of a powerful diesel held in check. Then abruptly that was reduced even further, and they heard a voice close by.

"Ahoy there!"

"Ahoy. *Silver Star* here." That was Donald MacInnes.

"You're blocking our way." The other boat must have come within metres of the fishing boat. "Please move aside and let us through."

"Sorry, I can't," said Donald cheerfully. "I've run aground."

"You've *what*?"

"Run aground. That means my bottom's on

159

the rocks. I can't move."

"I know damn well what it means. You've got to get off. We're in a hurry."

"I've tried. She won't budge. I'm afraid I'm here till the tide lifts me off."

"Like hell you are." A string of profanity ended suddenly in a charged silence. For a few moments they could hear nothing, then another voice spoke up, calm, unhurried.

"Give her another try, will you, skipper?"

Sandy nudged David. "That's Wally — I mean Ramshaw."

The polite request apparently mollified Donald. "Aye, I'll do that. You'll see."

The little craft's engine broke into life. The hull vibrated as the propeller churned the water at the stern. The boat shivered and shook, but she stayed where she was. Every minute the ebbing tide was leaving her more securely trapped.

The engine subsided. "She'll not budge," said Donald mildly. "Sorry to inconvenience you."

For a moment the two could hear nothing except for the deep rumble of the launch's idling motor, then Ramshaw spoke again, his voice still calm.

"How did you get into this predicament, skipper?"

"Just one of those things," replied Donald. "A wee bit careless, I'm afraid."

"I see. And where's your crew?"

160

David and Sandy looked at each other anxiously. "He's suspicious," whispered Sandy.

"Down having a cup of tea," said Donald easily. "Might as well. We're not going anywhere for a while."

Another pause, then Ramshaw spoke again. "You understand we have to get out of here, skipper. It's an emergency. Why don't we try to pull you off? We've got lots of power."

"Sorry, no." Donald spoke emphatically. "You'd tear the bottom out of her, or rip off the stanchion or whatever you hook on to."

"What if we offer to pay for any damages?"

"Do you have the cash with you?" There was a hint of sarcasm in Donald's voice.

Another pause, then Ramshaw said, "You'll have to think of something, skipper. I'll give you five minutes, then I'm coming aboard."

"We've got to do something," said David anxiously. "He might come down here. Even if he doesn't, it isn't natural for the crew to stay here while all this is going on. He'll begin to suspect."

"But we can't —" Sandy stopped. "But we *can*," she corrected herself, suddenly excited. "We can go up and clean the deck."

"What?"

"Don't you see? There are jellyfish on the deck. If we're going to get rid of them, we'll have to wear masks for protection."

"Of course! Masks, and oilskins too. Sandy, you're a genius!"

"I know," said Sandy modestly. "I do have my moments. Here's one for you. And look at this one. Mickey Mouse!" She hesitated before pulling it on. "You'll have to do the talking if we need to say anything. I sound too much like a girl."

"Strange but true," agreed David. "And I won't say any more than I have to in case Ramshaw recognizes my voice."

He pulled on one of the enveloping yellow oilskins, then a mask of an evil Dracula. I wish I had a mirror, he thought as he topped the ensemble with a floppy oilskin hat. He looked over at Sandy. Her large mouse ears helped to hold the oversize hat from coming down over her eyes. He laughed out loud.

"I can't believe this," he chuckled. "I just hope Ramshaw knows the custom of wearing these things."

"He might not, but Donald will back us up if he asks any questions. We'll have to chance it."

"Okay. But I hope those cops hurry up."

The twilight had finally given way to darkness when they emerged, but a powerful light from the launch bathed the deck in light. Donald was in the wheelhouse, leaning casually out the lowered window. They could see two figures on the launch where it nudged against the stern of the *Silver Star*. There was a moment of startled silence at their appearance, then a voice barked, "What's going on here?"

"Nothing to worry about," said Donald mildly.

"We've got some scalders on board that have to be cleaned up. The masks are worn to protect the face." Then to David and Sandy, "The broom's here, boys." He came out of the wheelhouse and handed a long-handled wire broom to David. "Might as well give the deck a good scrub down too."

He began to move the crates of lobsters, piling them to clear deck space. Sandy found a bucket, lowered it over the side, and sluiced sea water over the deck. David attacked it with the brush, pushing the water ahead of him. He didn't know where the jellyfish were, and was in no hurry to find out. The three of them converged at the bow.

"What do you think they'll do?" whispered David.

"What *can* they do?" wondered Donald.

"Perhaps they'll go back and get away by car," said Sandy hopefully. "Then they'll run into the police."

"Aye, perhaps."

They parted again. Sandy found one of the jellyfish. An involuntary "Ouch!" escaped her lips as she groped for it and a stinging tendril flicked her hand. David glanced at the launch, wondering if the unmistakably girlish voice had been heard. Apparently not, but the two on the launch didn't like being ignored. One of them stepped over the rail onto the *Silver Star*. It was Ramshaw.

"Come here, please. All of you." He spoke politely enough.

The three of them met him in front of the wheelhouse.

"We're in an emergency situation here," said Ramshaw. "We have to get out of this channel and you're in the way. We believe we could pull you off. Will you let us try?"

But Donald shook his head. "Not a chance," he said. "We're too firmly aground. You'll pull her apart."

"Then I'm afraid that's what we're going to have to do." The politeness had vanished from Ramshaw's voice. Suddenly there was a gun in his hand, directed at the three of them.

"Ho now!" Donald stepped back alarmed, bumping into the wheelhouse. His hands came up involuntarily. "What *is* this?"

"This is a revolver," said Ramshaw, icily calm. "And unless you co-operate I'm afraid I'm going to have to use it. We're either going to pull you off this rock or pull your boat to pieces, whatever it takes to get us out of this channel. And you're going to help us. Jake! The rope."

The man on the launch threw one end of a rope over the gunwale. The barbed hook in it landed on the deck.

"You two," snapped Ramshaw, waving his gun in the direction of the masked crew, "stand back against the wheelhouse with your hands in the air where I can see them. Now, skipper, it's up to you. If you want to save your boat, fasten that hook to something that'll hold, and be quick about it."

Donald shrugged in defeat. He pushed the gun aside and picked up the hook. "We'll have to pass it through the stern, then around the bitts," he said, "and hope you don't pull them up by the roots."

"Whatever, just get on with it. You," Ramshaw swung the gun onto David, "give him a hand. And take off that ridiculous mask!"

David's heart sank. What would Ramshaw do when he saw who was delaying him this time at his moment of escape? Would he remember that other time when they had thwarted his plans at the last minute? Of course he would. David felt cold fingers gripping his heart.

He glanced back past the launch, down the bay. There was a car coming, its lights sweeping back and forth as it negotiated the curves. But it was coming slowly, quietly. He wanted to see one coming fast, with siren wailing.

There was no alternative. He raised his hands to remove the mask. At the same time he stepped forward to help Donald, so that his back would be towards Ramshaw. He would delay the inevitable as long as possible.

As he moved he saw something that caused him to catch his breath in sudden hope. There was movement on the deck of the launch. Someone or something was edging forward in the shadow of the superstructure, someone who crouched and crept towards the man Ramshaw had called Jake.

"I'll lean over," Donald was saying, "and pass the rope back to you." He could have done it himself easily enough, but David went along with him, playing for time. He took the mask off, dropped it on the deck, and pulled the oilskin hat down low over his brow.

"Okay, Donald."

But there was no need to do any more. The silence was suddenly shattered by a wild scream. At the same moment David saw the crouched figure uncoil in a lightning movement to hurl itself against the unsuspecting Jake.

What was happening David had no idea. He only knew that Ramshaw must be, momentarily at least, off guard. Even as the unknown figure simultaneously screamed and sprang, David was turning. As Ramshaw's head snapped round in startled bewilderment towards the commotion, David launched himself forward, smashing into the gunman. Ramshaw fell back. The gunwale caught him behind the knees. His hands clawed desperately at David, yanking the hat from his head.

In the instant before he went over the side into the water, recognition dawned on Ramshaw's face. Recognition, amazement, and impotent fury.

David turned away, suddenly weak in the knees, and looked towards the launch. Jake was flat on his back. Standing over him was a wild figure, with a kilt and long white hair and beard.

"Good heavens," breathed David in awe. "Dugald MacGregor."

He was only dimly aware of the sound of approaching sirens.

18

"I think we've figured most of it out." Sandy was sitting beside David in Megan MacInnes's parlour, looking at the wild, unkempt figure of Dugald Mac-Gregor. "We may not have been correct in everything, but we must have been pretty close, the way things worked out. What we don't understand is how you came to be on that launch."

Dugald sighed. He was rubbing his wrists where they still bore the marks of rope burn. "I suppose you've guessed," he said, "that those diamonds were the ones paid to the Ramshaws centuries ago as ransom for a prisoner."

Sandy was just a little surprised. "We haven't had time to think about it," she said. "I'm sure we would have guessed it sooner or later though. But they were lost hundreds of years ago. Who found them?"

"Aulay MacLure. A long time ago, I think. And of course he turned them over to the Laird.

He knew that Ramshaw had never sold them, so when the Laird was taken to prison he thought they might still be hidden in the castle somewhere." Dugald took a drink from his tea cup and made a wry face. "I thought so too."

"You?" David looked at him curiously. "You knew about the diamonds?"

"I knew quite a bit about everything Ramshaw did or did not do." Dugald looked innocently at the ceiling. "To my advantage."

"You mean you blackmailed him?"

Dugald looked pained. "You have a blunt way of talking, young man. Blackmailers demand millions and get murdered. All I asked was a wee nip now and then, so I lived."

He put his booted feet on the coffee table, arranging his tattered kilt decorously over his legs. "When Ramshaw escaped he disguised himself as an American tourist and returned to the castle to get the diamonds — a nice nest egg to finance his future. It was a good disguise, but it didn't fool Aulay for long, so Aulay had to be put out of the way. What Ramshaw didn't know until too late was that Aulay had found the diamonds again and taken them from their hiding place."

Dugald chuckled. "That must have been a shock, eh? And then I recognized Wally Morrison for who he really was too."

"What gave him away?"

"The process of elimination. When Aulay died I guessed that Ramshaw was behind it and must be one of the guests. I've known him intimately for years. That night when I met you all in the lounge, I studied the guests and decided it had to be Wally. Then when he filled his pipe I knew for sure."

David nudged Sandy significantly. She kicked him on the ankle. "All right," she murmured, "don't gloat."

Dugald was continuing. "Unfortunately for me, I gave myself away somehow. Ramshaw knew that I recognized him, so he came after me when I left. I was talking to you on the telephone when *bam*! everything went black. He'd biffed me over the head.

"But my skull was thicker than he figured. When I came to I was in the back of his car, and he and Jake hadn't bothered to tie me up. So I opened the door and jumped out. That was no' such a good idea. I rolled and bounced for miles, so when they came back for me I was in no condition to put up much of a fight. I got my *sgian dhu* out of my sock, but Ramshaw grabbed it and flung it away."

"Into the cemetery," interjected David. "We found it there."

"Did you? Well, I was past caring. Next thing I knew I was their prisoner on that launch with Jake as my jailer, and this time they made no mistake about tying my hands and feet. But I bided my time and worked away at my bonds, and eventually they began to loosen. I got free a wee while ago, and tied up the woman in my place. Then I came out and did what I could on the deck. But I don't know if I could have done that much if you hadn't distracted Jake and Ramshaw. You came along just in time."

"You came along just in time for us too. What were they going to do with you?"

"They didn't say, but I don't think I would have lasted long if they had made it out to sea. Ramshaw had no intention of letting me — well, all right, blackmail him any more."

He looked across at Sandy and David. "He was angry with me, but that was nothing compared to the way he feels about you two. If he ever escapes again, you both ought to head for the South Pole."

"He won't," said Sandy, with a wide yawn. "And anyway, if he came in that door right now I'd ask him to please go away until the morning and we'd talk it over then. Davie, I think wo might actually get some sleep this time. We'd better — you start your job tomorrow."

He looked surprised. "My job! I'd forgotten." He frowned. "Somehow it won't be the same. I was looking forward to living with a ghost all summer."

"Never mind," she said, "you'll have to make do with me. But who knows, maybe the real ghost will return, just for you."